vowed

(book #7 in the vampire journals)

morgan rice

ISBN: 978-0-9829537-8-5

YA

Also by Morgan Rice

turned
(book #1 in the Vampire Journals)

loved
(Book #2 in the Vampire Journals)

betrayed
(Book #3 in the Vampire Journals)

destined
(Book #4 in the Vampire Journals)

desired
(Book #5 in the Vampire Journals)

betrothed
(Book #6 in the Vampire Journals)

FACT:

The remote Isle of Skye (Nordic for "the isle of mist"), located off the Western coast of Scotland, is an ancient place, where kings have lived and fought, where castles still exist, and where the most elite warriors trained for centuries.

FACT:

On the Isle of Skye, there exists a place in the landscape named Faerie Glen, where, it is said, if you make a wish, it must come true.

FACT:

Rosslyn Chapel, located in a small town in Scotland, is widely rumored to be the final resting place of the Holy Grail, rumored to be concealed behind a hidden wall, in a crypt in its lower levels.

"JULIET:
What satisfaction canst thou have to-night?

ROMEO:
The exchange of thy love's faithful vow for mine.

JULIET:
I gave thee mine before thou didst request it:
And yet I would it were to give again....
My bounty is as boundless as the sea,
My love as deep; the more I give to thee,
The more I have, for both are infinite."

--William Shakespeare, *Romeo and Juliet*

CHAPTER ONE

Highlands, Scotland
(1350)

Caitlin woke to a blood red sun. It filled the entire sky, a ball on the horizon, impossibly large. Standing against it was a lone silhouette, a figure she sensed could only be her father. He held out both arms, as if wanting her to run to him.

She desperately wanted to. But as she tried to sit up, she looked down and saw she was chained to a rock, iron clasps holding her wrists and feet in place. In one hand she held three keys—the keys she knew she needed to reach her father—and in the other, her necklace, its small silver cross dangling in her palm. She struggled as hard as she could, yet she could not move.

Caitlin blinked, and suddenly her father was standing over her, smiling down. She could feel the love radiating off of him. He knelt down, and gently unlocked her chains.

Caitlin leaned forward and hugged him, and she could feel his warmth, his reassurance. It felt so good to be in his arms; she could feel the tears pouring down her cheeks.

"I'm sorry, father. I let you down."

He pulled back and looked at her, smiling, as he stared directly into her eyes.

"You have done all I could have hoped for, and more," he answered. "Just one last key, and we will be together. Forever."

Caitlin blinked, and when she opened her eyes, he was gone.

In his place were two figures, lying motionless on a rocky plateau. Caleb and Scarlet.

Suddenly, Caitlin remembered. Their sickness.

She tried to move from the rock, but she was still chained, and struggle as she did, she couldn't reach them. She blinked, and Scarlet suddenly stood over her, looking down.

"Mommy?" she asked.

Scarlet smiled down at her, and Caitlin could feel her love enveloping her. She wanted to hug her, and she struggled for all she had, but she could not break free.

"Mommy?" Scarlet asked again, reaching out a single, small hand.

Caitlin sat bolt upright.

Breathing hard, she ran her hands along her sides, trying to figure out if she were still chained, or if she were free. She moved her hands and feet freely, and looked around, and saw no signs of chains. She looked up, and saw a huge, blood-red sun sitting on the horizon, then looked around, and saw that she was lying on a rocky plateau. Just as in her dream.

Dawn was just breaking over the horizon. As far as she could see were mountain peaks, covered in mist, endlessly beautiful against the open sky. She peered into the muted light of dawn, trying to make out her surroundings, and as she did, her heart leapt. There, lying in the distance, were two figures, unmoving. She could already sense who it was: Caleb and Scarlet.

Caitlin jumped to her feet and ran over to them, kneeling between them, reaching out one hand to each of their chests, shaking them lightly. Her heart pounded with fear as she struggled to remember the events of their previous incarnation. Horrific image after image flashed through her mind, as she remembered how sick they had been, Scarlet covered in boils from smallpox, and Caleb dying from vampire poison. Last she had seen them, it had seemed certain that they would both die.

Caitlin reached down and felt her own neck, felt the two small scars. She recalled that final, fateful moment when Caleb had fed on her. Had it worked? Had it brought him back?

Caitlin shook each one frantically.

"Caleb!" she cried. "Scarlet!"

Caitlin felt tears well up, as she tried not to think about what life would be like without them. It was too much to even contemplate. If they could not be with her, then she would rather not go on.

Suddenly, Scarlet moved. Caitlin's heart soared with hope as she watched her shift and then slowly, gradually, reach up and rub her eyes. She looked up at Caitlin, and Caitlin could see her skin was completely healed, her small, blue eyes bright and shining.

Scarlet broke into a wide smile, and Caitlin's heart lifted.

"Mommy!" Scarlet said. "Where were you?"

Caitlin burst into tears of joy, as she reached down and pulled Scarlet to her, holding her. Over her shoulder, she said, "I'm right here, sweetheart."

"I was dreaming that I couldn't find you," she said. "And that I was sick."

Caitlin breathed with relief, sensing that Scarlet was completely healed.

"It was just a bad dream," Caitlin said. "You're okay now. Everything is going to be okay."

There was a sudden barking, and Caitlin turned to see Ruth charging around the corner, right for them. She was overjoyed to see that she had made it back, too, and amazed to see how large Ruth had grown, now a full-size wolf.

Yet Ruth still acted like a puppy, wagging her tail excitedly, as she ran into Scarlet's arms.

"Ruth!" Scarlet screamed, peeling away from Caitlin, and hugging her.

Ruth could barely contain her excitement, charging her with such force, that she knocked Scarlet over.

Scarlet bounced back up, screaming with laughter and delight.

"What's all the commotion?" came a voice.

Caleb.

Caitlin wheeled, feeling a thrill at the sound of Caleb's voice. He was standing over her, smiling. She couldn't believe it. He looked so young and healthy, better than she'd ever seen him.

She jumped up and gave him a hug, so grateful he was alive. She felt his strong muscles as he hugged her back, and it felt so good to be in his arms again. Finally, everything was right in the world. It had been like a long, bad dream.

"I was so scared you had died," Caitlin said, over his shoulder.

She leaned back and looked at him.

"Do you remember?" she asked. "Do you remember being sick?"

He furrowed his brow.

"Vaguely," he answered. "It all feels like a dream. I remember...seeing Jade. And...feeding on you." Suddenly Caleb looked at her, eyes wide. "You saved me," he said, awestruck.

He leaned in and hugged her.

"I love you," she whispered into his ear, as he held her.

"I love you, too," he answered.

"Daddy!"

Caleb lifted Scarlet in a huge embrace. He then reached down and petted Ruth, as did Caitlin.

Ruth couldn't be happier with all the attention, jumping up and whining, trying to hug them back.

After some time, Caleb took Caitlin's hand and together they turned and looked out over the horizon. A soft, morning light filled the endless sky before them, mountain peaks punctuating the horizon, the rose-colored light swirling through the mist. The peaks stretched on forever, and looking down, she could see that they were at an elevation of thousands of feet. She wondered where on earth they could be.

"I was wondering the same thing," Caleb said, reading her thoughts.

They surveyed the horizon, turning completely in every direction.

"Do you recognize it?" Caitlin asked.

He slowly shook his head.

"Well, it looks like we only have two options," she continued. "Up or down. We're so high up already, I say we go up. Let's see what's to be seen from the top."

Caleb nodded his approval, Caitlin reached out and took Scarlet's hand, and the three of them began to hike up the slope.

It was cold up here, and Caitlin was barely dressed for this weather. She still had on her black leather boots, her tightly fitting black pants, and a fitted black long-sleeved shirt, from her sparring time in England. But it wasn't warm enough to shield her from these cold, mountain winds.

They pressed on, climbing up the slope, grabbing onto boulders and pulling their way up.

As the sun rose higher in the sky, just as she was beginning to wonder if they'd made the right decision, finally, they reached the highest peak.

Out of breath, they stopped and surveyed their surroundings, finally able to see over the ridge.

The sight took Caitlin's breath away. There, spread out before them, was the other side of the mountain range, stretching as far as the eye could see. Beyond that, an ocean. Far out into the ocean, she could see a mountainous, rocky island, covered in green. A primordial island, jutting out from the ocean, it was more picturesque than anything she had ever seen. It looked like a place of fairytales, especially in the early morning light, covered in an eerie mist, and in an orange and purple glow.

Even more dramatic, the only thing connecting the island to the mainland was an endlessly long rope bridge, which swayed violently in the wind and looked hundreds of years old. Beneath it was a drop of hundreds of feet to the ocean.

"Yes," Caleb said. "That is it. That island is familiar." He surveyed it in awe.

"Where are we?" Caitlin asked.

He looked out at the sight with reverence, then turned and faced her, excitement in his eyes.

"Skye," he said to her. "The legendary Isle of Skye. Home to warriors, and to our kind, for thousands of years. We are in Scotland, then," he said. "near the approach to Skye. Clearly, that is where we are meant to go. It is a sacred place."

"Let's fly," Caitlin said, feeling her wings already active.

Caleb shook his head.

"Skye is one of the few places on earth where that is not possible. There will surely be vampire warriors guarding it, and more importantly, there will be an energy shield protecting it from direct overhead flight. The water creates a psychic barrier to this place. No vampire can enter without being invited." He turned and looked at her. "We're going to have to enter the hard way: by crossing that rope bridge."

Caitlin stared at the bridge, swaying in the wind.

"But that bridge is treacherous," she said.

Caleb sighed.

"Skye is unlike any other place. Only the worthy are allowed to enter. Most people who try to approach it, meet their deaths, in one way or another."

Caleb looked at her.

"We can turn back," he offered.

Caitlin thought about it, then shook her head.

"No," she answered, determined. "We were placed here for a reason. Let's do it."

CHAPTER TWO

Sam woke with a start. His world was spinning, then rocking violently, and he couldn't understand where he was, or what was happening. He was lying on his back, that much he knew, on what felt like wood, slumped in an uncomfortable position. He was looking straight up at the sky, and he saw the clouds moving erratically.

Sam reached over, grabbed hold of a piece of wood, and pulled himself up. He sat there, blinking, his world still spinning, and got a hold of his surroundings. He couldn't believe it. He was on a boat, a small, wooden rowboat, lying on the floor, in the middle of an ocean.

It rocked violently in the rough sea, the waves lifting it and bringing it back down. It creaked and groaned as it moved, bobbing up and down, rocking side to side. Sam saw the foam of the waves crashing all around him, felt the cold, salty wind spray him in his hair and on his face. It was early morning, in fact, a beautiful dawn, with the sky breaking in a myriad of colors. He wondered how on earth he had ended up here.

Sam spun around and surveyed the boat, and as he did, he spotted a figure lying there, in the dim morning light, on the far side, curled up, on the floor, and covered with a shawl. He wondered who it could be, stuck with him on this small boat in the middle of nowhere. And then he sensed it. It went through him, like an electric shock. He didn't have to see her face.

Polly.

Every bone in Sam's body told him. He was surprised at how definitively he knew, at how connected he was with her, how deep his feelings ran for her—almost as if they were one. He didn't understand how it had happened so quickly.

As he sat there, looking at her, unmoving, he suddenly felt a feeling of dread. He couldn't tell if she were alive or not, and at that moment, he realized how devastated he would be if she were not. That was when he realized, finally, unequivocally, that he loved her.

Sam got to his feet, stumbling in the small boat as a wave turned and lifted it, and managed to take a few steps and kneel by her side. He reached over and gently pulled back the shawl, and shook her shoulders. She didn't respond, and his heart pounded as he waited.

"Polly?" he asked.

No reply.

"*Polly*," he said, more firmly. "Wake up. It's me, Sam."

But she didn't budge, and as Sam brushed the bare skin of her shoulder, it felt too cold to him. His heart stopped. Could it be possible?

Sam leaned over and held her face in his hands. She was as beautiful as he remembered, her skin a very pale shade of translucent white, her hair a light brown, and her perfectly-chiseled features exquisite in the glow of the early morning light. He saw her perfect, full lips, her small nose, her large eyes, her long, brown hair. He remembered those eyes when they were open, an incredible, crystal blue, like the ocean. He longed to see them open again now; he would do anything. He longed to see her smile, to hear her voice, her laughter. In the past, it had sometimes bothered him when she talked too much. But now, he would give anything to hear her talk forever.

But her skin was too cold in his hands. Ice cold. And he was beginning to despair that her eyes would never open again.

"Polly!" he screamed, and as he did, he could hear the despair in his own voice, as it rose to the sky, and blended with the screech of a bird overhead.

Sam was growing desperate. He had no idea what to do. He was shaking her harder and harder, but she was just not responding. He thought back to the time and place he had last seen her. Sergei's palace. He remembered freeing her. They had gone back, to Aiden's castle, and had found Caitlin and Caleb and Scarlet, all lying lifeless on that bed. Aiden had told him that they had gone back in time, without them. He had implored Aiden to send them back, too. Aiden had shook his head, saying it was not meant to be, that it would interfere with destiny. But Sam had insisted.

Finally, Aiden had performed the ritual.

Had she died on the trip back?

Sam looked down and shook Polly again. Still nothing.

Finally, Sam reached down and pulled Polly close to him. He pulled her long, beautiful hair out of her face, placed one hand back behind her neck, and pulled her face close. He leaned down and kissed her.

It was a long, full kiss, planted fully on her lips, and Sam realized then, that this was only the second time they had ever really kissed. Her lips felt so soft, so perfect in his. But also too cold, too devoid of life. As he kissed her, he tried to focus on sending his love through her, on willing her back to life. In his mind, he tried to send a clear message. *I'll do anything. I'll pay whatever price. I'll do anything to have you back. Just come back to me.*

"I'LL PAY ANY PRICE!" Sam leaned back and screamed to the waves.

The scream seemed to rise into the heavens, and as it did, it was echoed back by a flock of birds, flying overhead. Sam felt a chill run through his body, as he sensed, at that moment, that the universe had heard and answered him. He knew at that moment, with every ounce of his body, that Polly would, indeed, come back to life. Even though she wasn't meant to. That he had willed it to happen, had broken some greater plan in the universe. And that he would, indeed, pay the price.

Suddenly, Sam looked down, and watched as Polly's eyes opened slowly. They were as blue and beautiful as he had remembered, and they were staring right at him. For a moment they were blank, but then they filled with recognition. And then, the greatest magic he had ever seen, a small smile formed at the corner of her lips.

"Are you trying to take advantage of a girl while she's asleep?" Polly asked, in her typical, jovial voice.

Sam couldn't help but break into a huge grin. Polly was back. Nothing else mattered. He tried to push out of his mind the ominous feeling that he had defied destiny, that he would have to pay the price.

Polly sat up, back to her nimble, happy self, looking embarrassed to have been caught so vulnerable in his arms, and trying to make a show of being strong and independent. She took in her surroundings, and grabbed onto the side of the boat as a wave brought them high, then lurched them low.

"This isn't exactly what I would call a romantic boating expedition," she said, looking a bit pale as she tried to steady herself in the rocking sea. "Where are we exactly? And what is that on the horizon?"

Sam turned and looked where she was pointing. He hadn't seen it before. There, a few hundred yards off in the distance, sat a rocky island, jutting straight out of the sea, with tall, unforgiving cliffs. It looked ancient, uninhabited, its terrain rocky and desolate.

He turned and surveyed the horizon in every direction. It looked like the only island within thousands of miles.

"It looks like we're heading right for it," he said.

"I sure hope so," Polly said. "I'm positively nauseous on this boat."

Suddenly, Polly leaned over the side and threw up, again and again.

Sam came over and placed a reassuring hand on her back. Polly finally stood, wiping her mouth with the back of her sleeve and looking away, embarrassed.

"Sorry," she said. "These waves are relentless." She looked up at him, guiltily. "It must be unattractive."

But Sam wasn't thinking that at all. On the contrary, he was realizing that he had stronger feelings for Polly than he ever realized.

"Why are you looking at me like that?" Polly asked. "Was it that awful?"

Sam quickly looked away, realizing he was staring.

"I wasn't thinking that at all," he said, blushing.

But they were both interrupted. On the island there suddenly appeared several warriors, standing at the top of a cliff. One appeared after another, and soon the horizon was filled with them.

Sam reached down, searching to see what weapons he had brought with him. But he was disappointed to find he had not brought any.

The horizon blackened with more and more vampire warriors, and Sam could see that the current was bringing them right to them. They were drifting right into a trap, and there was nothing they could do to stop it.

"Look at that," Polly said. "They're coming to greet us."

Sam studied them carefully, and came to a very different conclusion.

"No they're not," he said. "They're coming to test us."

CHAPTER THREE

Caitlin stood before the rope bridge to Skye, Caleb beside her, and Scarlet and Ruth behind them. She watched the dilapidated rope sway violently, as she heard the wind whistling through the rocks, the waves crashing against the cliffs hundreds of feet below. The bridge was wet and slippery. Slipping off it would mean instant death for Scarlet and for Ruth, and Caitlin hadn't tested her own wings yet, either. Crossing this bridge was not really a chance she wanted to take—but then again, it seemed obvious that they needed to be on the Isle of Skye.

Caleb looked over at her.

"We haven't much choice," he said.

"Then there's no point in waiting," she answered. "I'll take Scarlet, you take Ruth?"

Caleb nodded grimly back, as Caitlin picked up Scarlet and hoisted her onto her back, while Caleb held Ruth in his arms. Ruth at first squirmed, wanting to get down, but Caleb held her firmly, and something about his grip eventually calmed her.

There was no choice but to walk single file on the narrow bridge. Caitlin went first.

Caitlin took her first, unsteady step onto the bridge, and could immediately feel how slippery the water-sprayed planks were. She reached over and grabbed the rope railing for balance, but the bridge only swayed as she did, and the railing fell to pieces in her hands.

She closed her eyes, took a deep breath, and centered herself. She knew she could not rely on her vision, or her balance. She had to call on something deeper. She thought back to Aiden's lessons, summoned his words. She stopped trying to oppose the bridge: instead, she tried to feel at one with it.

Caitlin trusted her inner instincts, and took several steps forward. She slowly opened her eyes, and as she took another step, a plank fell through beneath her. Scarlet cried out, and she lost her balance for a moment—then quickly took another step and found her footing. The wind swayed the bridge again. It felt like she had been going forever, but when Caitlin looked up, she saw they had only gone about ten feet. She knew instinctively that they would never make it.

She turned and looked at Caleb. She could see the look in his eyes, and knew that he was thinking the same thing. She wanted more than anything to just spread her wings and take off, but as she felt them, she sensed something in the air, and knew that Caleb had been right: there was some sort of invisible energy shield up around this island, and flying here uninvited would not work.

The wind blew the bridge again, and Caitlin was beginning to feel desperate. They had gone too far to turn back.

She made a split-second decision.

"On three, jump off, grab your side of the railing, and let it swing you all the way!" she suddenly called out to Caleb. "It's the only way!"

"What if it gives!?" he screamed back.

"We have no choice! If we continue as we are, we will die!"

Caleb didn't argue.

"ONE!" she yelled, taking a deep breath, "TWO! THREE!"

She leapt into the air, off to her right, and saw Caleb leap to his left. She could hear Scarlet screaming and Ruth whining as they were falling over the edge. She reached up and grabbed hard on the rope railing, praying to God that it would hold true this time. She saw Caleb doing the same.

A second later, they were holding onto the rope and swinging through the air, at full speed, the saltwater rising up from the waves and crashing over them. For a moment, Caitlin couldn't tell if they were still swinging, or falling straight down.

But after a few seconds, she could feel the tension of the rope catching in her hand, and felt them not plummeting straight down, but rather swinging towards the far cliff. It was holding.

Caitlin braced herself. The rope was holding, and that was good. But they were also swinging fast, right for the side of the cliff. Smashing into it, she knew, would be painful.

She turned her shoulder and positioned Scarlet behind her, so that she could take the full force of the blow. She looked over and saw Caleb doing the same, holding Ruth with one arm behind him, and leaning in with his shoulder. They both braced for impact.

A second later, they crashed hard into the wall, with a flood of pain. The force of the impact knocked the wind out of Caitlin, and she was momentarily stunned. But she still held onto the rope, and she could see that Caleb did, too. She hung there, dazed for several seconds, checking to see if Scarlet was okay, and if Caleb was. They were.

Caitlin slowly stopped seeing stars, and eventually she reached up, and started to pull herself up the rope, straight up the face of the cliff. She looked up, and saw she had thirty yards to go before reaching the top. She then made the mistake of turning and looking down: it was a perilous drop, and she realized that if the rope gave way, they would plummet hundreds of feet into the sharp rocks below.

Caleb recovered and was climbing straight up his rope, too. The two of them were making good speed, even while slipping on the mossy cliffs.

Suddenly, Caitlin heard a sickening noise. It was the sound of rope snapping.

Caitlin braced herself for a moment, preparing to plummet to her death, but then realized she didn't feel her rope giving way. She looked over immediately, and saw that it was Caleb's.

His rope was snapping.

Caitlin jumped into action. She kicked off the rock, and swung her rope closer to him, reaching out a free hand. She managed to grab Caleb's hand just as he was plummeting to earth. She held it tight with her free hand, holding him there, dangling in the air. Then, with a supreme effort, she lifted him up several feet, into a deep crevice in the side of the cliff. Caleb, still holding Ruth, was able to stand firmly on a ledge, and to grab hold of a natural handle inside the rock face.

Secure, she could see the relief on his face.

But there was no time to reflect. Caitlin immediately turned and hurried up the rope.

Her rope could snap, too, at any moment, and she still had Scarlet on her back.

Finally, she reached the top. She quickly jumped up onto the grassy plateau and deposited Scarlet. She felt so grateful to be on steady land—but she didn't waste any time. She rolled over, took the rope, and threw it hard several feet, so that it swung over to where Caleb was standing, below.

She looked down and saw that he was watching carefully for it, and as it came his way, he reached out and grabbed it, holding Ruth with the other hand. He managed to pull them up quickly, too. Caitlin watched carefully his every step, praying that it would not give.

Finally, he made it to the top, rolling over onto the grass, right beside her. They scurried far from the ledge, and as they did, Scarlet and Ruth embraced, and Caitlin and Caleb did the same.

Caitlin could feel the relief flooding her body, as it did his.

"You saved my life," he said. "Again."

She shot back a smile.

"You saved mine many times," she said. "I owe you at least a few."

He smiled back.

They all turned and surveyed their new surroundings. The Isle of Skye. It was gorgeous, breathtaking, mystical, desolate and dramatic at the same time. The island curved in a series of mountains and valleys and hills and plateaus, some of it rocky and barren, some of it covered in a green moss. It was all shrouded by a heavenly mist, which made its way into the nooks and cracks, and was lit up orange and red and yellow in the morning sun. This island looked like a place of dreams. And it also looked like a place that no humans could ever possibly live.

As she watched the horizon, suddenly, like an apparition, a dozen vampires walked out of the mist, over the hill, appearing slowly, heading right for them. Caitlin could not believe it. She braced herself for battle, but Caleb reached over and placed a reassuring hand on hers, as they all stood.

"Don't worry," Caleb said. "I can sense it. They are friendly."

As they got closer, Caitlin could see their features, and sensed that he was right. In fact, she was shocked at what she saw.

Standing there, before her, were several of her old friends.

CHAPTER FOUR

Sam braced himself as their boat, rocking wildly, propelled itself inevitably toward the rocky shore. He could feel Polly's apprehension, as dozens of vampire warriors scurried down the steep cliffs, heading towards them.

"Now what?" Polly asked, their boat just feet from shore.

"No other way," Sam answered. "We make our stand."

With those words, he suddenly leapt off the boat, holding Polly's hand, taking her with him. The two of them leapt several feet in the air, landing at the water's edge. Sam felt the shock of the icy cold water on his bare feet; it sent a shiver up his spine, waking him completely. He realized he was still clothed in his battle gear from London—tight black pants and shirt, thickly padded around the shoulders and arms, and he looked over and realized that Polly was, too.

But there wasn't much time to take in anything else. As Sam looked to the shore, he saw dozens of human warriors charging towards them. Dressed in chain mail armor from head to toe, wielding swords, carrying shields, they were the classic vision of knights in shining armor that Sam had seen in picture books all throughout his childhood—the knights he had once wanted to be. As a child, he'd idolized them. But now, being a vampire, he knew he was so much stronger than they would ever be. He knew they could never possibly match the strength or speed that he did, never come close to his fighting skills. So Sam wasn't afraid.

But he was very much protective of Polly. He wasn't quite sure how evolved Polly's fighting skills were, and he didn't entirely like the look of these humans weapons. They were unlike any other swords and shields he had seen. He could already see, gleaming in the morning sun, that they appeared to be silver-tipped. Designed to kill vampires.

He knew it was a threat he had to take seriously.

From the looks on their faces, these humans meant business and he could see from their tight, coordinated formations that they were well-trained. For humans, these were probably the best warriors of this time. They were well organized, too, charging from both directions.

Sam wouldn't give them the advantage of the first strike.

Sam charged them himself, breaking into a sprint, suddenly approaching them faster than they were him.

Clearly, they hadn't expected this. He could sense their hesitation, unsure how to react.

But he didn't give them any time. With one flying leap, he leapt over their heads, using his wings to propel him, until he cleared the entire group, and landed behind them. As he did, he reached down and grabbed a lance from a rear knight. As he landed, he swung it wide, knocking several of them off of their horses in one motion.

The horses neighed and kicked, charging the rest of the group, and causing chaos.

Still, these knights were well trained, and did not let it faze them. Any other human knights would have dispersed immediately, but these, to Sam's surprise, turned and re-grouped, forming a single line and charging for Sam.

Sam was surprised at this, and wondered exactly where he was. Had he landed in some sort of elite warrior kingdom?

Sam didn't have time to figure it out. And he didn't want to kill these humans. Part of him sensed that they weren't out to kill; he felt they were out to confront, and maybe, to capture them. Or, more likely, to test them. After all, they had landed on their turf: he sensed that they wanted to see what they were made of.

Sam had, at least, succeeded in diverting them from Polly. Now they charged only for him.

He reached back with the lance, and aimed for the shield of their leader, wanting to stun but not kill him, and threw it.

A direct hit. He knocked the shield clean out of his hand, and knocked him off of his horse. The knight landed with a loud clang of metal.

Sam jumped forward and grabbed the sword and shield from the knight's hands. Just in time, as several blows descended upon him. He blocked them all, and as he did, tore a mace from another knight's hands. He grabbed on the long wooden shaft, reached back, and swung the deadly metal ball and chain in a wide arc. There was the clang of metal in every direction, as Sam managed to knock swords out of the hands of a dozen warriors. He continued swinging, hitting several on their shields and knocking them to the ground.

But again, Sam was surprised. Any other human warriors would surely have dispersed in chaos; but not these men. Those who had been knocked off their horses, dazed, regrouped, grabbed their weapons off the sand, and formed around Sam, encircling him. This time, they kept a greater distance, enough of a distance that Sam couldn't reach them with the mace.

More distressing, they all, from every direction, suddenly extracted crossbows off their backs, and aimed right for him. Sam could see they were loaded with silver-tip arrows. All meant to kill. Perhaps he had been too lenient with them.

They didn't fire, but they held him in their deadly sites. Sam realized he was in a bind. He couldn't believe it. Any rash move could be his last.

"Drop your bows," came a cold, steely voice.

The humans slowly turned their heads, and Sam turned his, too.

He couldn't believe it. Standing there, on the outer perimeter of the circle, was Polly. She held one of the soldiers in a deadly embrace, her forearm wrapped around his throat and holding a small silver dagger to his throat. The soldier stood there, frozen, unable to move in Polly's grip, his eyes wide with fear, the look of a man about to die.

"If not," Polly continued, "this man dies."

Sam was stunned by the tone of her voice. He'd never seen Polly as a warrior, never seen her so cold and firm. It was like looking at a whole new person, and he was impressed.

The humans, apparently, were impressed, too. Slowly, reluctantly, they dropped their crossbows, one by one, onto the sand.

"Off your horses," she commanded.

Slowly, each one obeyed, dismounting. The dozens of human warriors stood there, at Polly's mercy as she held the man hostage.

"So. The girl saves the boy, does she?" suddenly came a loud, joyful voice. It was followed by a deep, hearty laughter, and all heads turned.

From out of nowhere there appeared a human warrior, mounted on a horse, draped in furs, wearing a crown, and flanked by a dozen more soldiers. Clearly, from the look of him, he was their king. He had wild, orange hair, a thick, orange beard, and glowing, mischievous green eyes. He leaned back and laughed heartily, as he took in the scene before him.

"Impressive," he continued, seeming amused by the whole thing. "Very impressive, indeed."

He dismounted, and as he did, all his men immediately parted ways, as he walked into the circle. Sam felt himself redden, as he realized that it must have looked as if he were unable to handle himself, as if he would have been helpless if it weren't for Polly. Which was, he realized, at least partly, true. But he couldn't be too upset, because at the same time, he was so grateful to her for saving him.

Furthering his embarrassment, the King ignored him, and walked right up to Polly.

"You can let him go now," the King said to her, still smiling.

"Why should I?" she asked, looking back and forth from him to Sam, still cautious.

"Because we were never going to hurt you. It was but a test. To see if you were worthy of being on Skye. After all," he laughed, "you landed on *our* shores!"

The King broke into hearty laughter again, and several of his men stepped forward, handing him two long, bejeweled swords, gleaming in the morning light, cover with rubies and sapphires and emeralds. Sam was taken aback at the sight: they were the most beautiful swords he had ever seen.

"You have passed our test," the King announced. "And these are for you. A gift."

Sam walked over to Polly's side, as she slowly let go her hostage. They each reached out, and took a sword, examining the jewel-encrusted hilt. Sam marveled at its craftsmanship.

"For two very worthy warriors," he said. "We are honored to welcome you."

He turned his back, and began to walk, and it was clear that Sam and Polly were meant to follow. As he walked, he boomed out:

"Welcome to our Isle of Skye."

CHAPTER FIVE

Caitlin and Caleb, followed by Scarlet and Ruth, walked at a brisk pace through the Isle of Skye, flanked by Taylor, Tyler, and several other of Aiden's coven members. Caitlin was overjoyed to see them. After the initial hardships of landing in this place and time, she finally felt a sense of peace and ease, as she knew they were exactly where they were supposed to be. Taylor and Tyler, and all of Aiden's people, had been thrilled to see them, too. It was so odd seeing them in this different time and place, in this cold climate, on this stark and barren island in the middle of nowhere. Caitlin was beginning to see how times and places changed, but people were timeless.

Taylor and Tyler led them on a brisk walking tour of the island, and they had been walking for hours. Caitlin had asked immediately if they had any news of Sam or Polly; when they had said no, she had been crestfallen. She desperately hoped that they'd made it back in time, too.

As they walked, Taylor filled them in on their coven's rituals, habits, new training methods, and on anything and everything Caitlin could possibly want to know. Caitlin realized that Skye was stunning, one of the most beautiful places she had ever been. It felt ancient, primordial, with boulders rising from the landscape, moss-covered hills, mountain lakes reflecting the morning sun, and a beautiful mist which seemed to hang over everything.

"The mist never leaves us," Tyler said, smiling, reading Caitlin's mind.

Caitlin blushed, embarrassed, as always, at how easily others read her thoughts.

"In fact, that's where it gets its name: Skye means 'the misty isle,'" Taylor said. "It lends a pretty dramatic backdrop to everything here, don't you think?"

Caitlin nodded, surveying the landscape.

"And it's useful in battling our enemies," Tyler chimed in. "Yet no one even dares approach our shores."

"I don't blame them," Caleb said. "That was hardly a welcoming entrance."

Taylor and Tyler smiled.

"Only the worthy can approach. That's our test. It's been years since anyone's tried to visit—and even more years since they passed that test and made it to our shores alive."

"Only the worthy can survive and train here," Taylor said. "But the training is the best in the world."

"Skye is an unforgiving place," Tyler added, "a place of extremes. Aiden's coven is as close here as it's ever been. We hardly ever leave. We train together nearly all day long, and in the most extreme of environments—cold, fog, rain, cliffs, in the mountains, on freezing lakes, on rocky shores—sometimes even in the ocean. There are very few training methods he hasn't put us through. And we are more battle-hardened than we have ever been."

"And we do not train alone," Tyler added. "Human warriors live here, too, led by their King, McCleod. They have a castle and their own legion of warriors, and we all live and train together. It is very unusual, vampires and humans training together. But we are very close here. We are all warriors, and we all respect the warrior code."

"Although, of course," Tyler said, "we don't cross any lines with mating. Many of them would like to have our vampire skills, but Aiden has strict rules about our turning humans. So they are resigned to the fact that they never will be one of us. We live and train in harmony together. We sharpen their skills beyond what any human could dream of. And they offer us shelter and protection. They have an arsenal of silver-tipped weapons, and if any rival covens should ever attack, they stand ready to defend us."

"A castle?" Scarlet suddenly asked. "A real castle?"

Taylor looked down, and broke into a big smile. She reached over and took Scarlet's free hand as they walked.

"Yes, love. We are bringing you there right now. In fact," she said, as they rounded a hill and pointed, "it's just over there."

They all stopped and stared, and Caitlin was amazed at the sight. Before them was an expansive vista of rolling hills, mountains, lakes, and in the distance, perched on its own small cliff, was an ancient castle, nestled at the edge of a huge lake.

"Dunvegan Castle," Taylor announced. "Home of Scottish kings for centuries."

"WOW!" Scarlet screamed. "Mommy, we get to live in a castle!"

Caitlin couldn't help but smile, as did the others, as Scarlet's enthusiasm was infectious.

"Can Ruth come, too!?" Scarlet asked. Caitlin glanced at Taylor, who nodded back. "Of course she can, love."

Scarlet squealed in delight, hugging Ruth, and the group hurried down the slope, towards the distant castle.

As Caitlin surveyed the castle, she sensed that some deep secrets lay within its walls, secrets that could help her on her search for her father. Once again, she sensed that she was in exactly the right place.

"Is Aiden here?" Caitlin asked Tyler.

"That's what we've been wondering for a while now," Tyler answered. "I haven't seen him in weeks. Sometimes he disappears for a while. You know how he is."

Caitlin did, indeed. She thought back to all the times, all the places she had been with them. She desperately needed to talk to him now, to know more about why they had landed in this place and time, to find out if Sam and Polly were okay, to find out about the final key—and most of all, if her father was here now. She had so many burning questions she was dying to ask him. Like, what had happened in London before they were all sent back? Had Kyle managed to survive?

As they approached the castle, Caitlin looked up and admired its architecture—rising fifty feet high, it sprawled over many levels, in a rectangular shape, with several square towers and parapets. It sat boldly and proudly at the top of a cliff, overlooking the vast lake and open sky, and unlike other castles, it was bright and airy, with dozens of windows. Its approach was impressive, with a wide stone roadway leading up to a front gate and an imposing arched doorway. This was clearly not a place one approached easily, and as Caitlin looked up, she spotted human guards on all the towers, watching them like a hawk.

As they approached the entrance, there was suddenly a sounding of trumpets, followed by the rumble of horses' hooves.

Caitlin turned. Galloping over the horizon, rushing right towards them, were dozens of human warriors, dressed in armor. Leading them was an imposing man dressed in furs, with a large orange beard, flanked by attendants, and bearing the demeanor of a king. He had soft facial features, and seemed to be the type who smiled easily. He had a large entourage of warriors, and Caitlin would have tensed up, if it weren't for Taylor and Tyler being so relaxed. Clearly, these were friends.

As the soldiers stopped before them and parted ways, Caitlin stopped in her tracks, shocked.

There, in the center of the group, dismounting, were two people she loved most in the world. She couldn't believe it. She blinked several times. It was really them.

Standing before her, grinning back, were Sam and Polly.

*

Caitlin and Sam each stepped forward before the two large groups of warriors and met in a huge embrace. Caitlin felt so relieved to be holding her brother, to be hugging him, to see and feel that he was alive, and really here. She then leaned over and hugged Polly, as Caleb, too, stepped up, and gave both Sam and Polly a hug.

"Polly!" Scarlet cried, as she came running up, Ruth barking by her side. Polly knelt down and gave her a huge hug, picking her up in her arms.

"I didn't think I'd ever see you again!" Scarlet said.

Polly beamed. "You can't get rid of me that easily!"

Ruth barked, and Polly knelt down and hugged her, while Sam hugged Scarlet.

Caitlin felt herself basking in the warm glow of having her family and loved ones reunited. She thought back to London, to everyone sick and dying, to the time when she couldn't imagine that a happy scene like this would ever be possible. She felt so grateful that everything seemed to be restored, and marveled at how many lifetimes she had already led. It made her so grateful for immortality. She couldn't imagine what she would do with just one life.

"What happened to guys?" Caitlin asked Sam. "Last I saw you, you promised me you wouldn't leave Caleb and Scarlet's side. And when I returned, you were gone."

Caitlin was still upset at their betrayal.

Sam and Polly looked down in shame.

"I'm so sorry," Sam said. "It was my fault. Polly was abducted, and I left to save her."

"No, it's my fault," Polly said. "Sergei had said there was a cure, and that I had to go with him to get it. I was so stupid—I believed him. I thought I would save them. But I broke my promise to you. Will you ever forgive me?"

"And me?" Sam asked.

Caitlin looked at both their faces, and could see their absolute sincerity. A part of her was still upset that they'd broke their word and left Scarlet and Caleb so open to attack. But another part of her, the part that was evolving, was telling her to completely forgive them and let it go.

She took a deep breath, and focused on letting it go. She exhaled, and nodded.

"Yes, I forgive you both," she said.

They both smiled back.

"*You* might forgive them," King McCleod suddenly said, dismounting and stepping towards them, "but *I* don't forgive them for embarrassing my men like that!" he said, letting out a hearty laugh. "Especially Polly. The two of you put my finest warriors to shame. Clearly, we have a lot to learn from you, as we have learned from the others. Vampires versus humans.

Never fair," he said, shaking his head, with another hearty laugh.

McCleod stepped forward and approached Caitlin and Caleb. Caitlin liked him immediately. He was quick to smile, had a deep, comforting laugh, and seemed to put everyone at ease around him.

"Welcome to our island," he said, reaching up, taking Caitlin's hand and kissing it with a bow. He then reached over and shook Caleb's hand warmly in both of his. "The Isle of Skye. There is no place like it on earth. Desperate home to the greatest warriors. This castle has been in my family for hundreds of years. You'll stay with us. Aiden will be thrilled. As will my men. I officially welcome you!" he said with a shout, and all his men cheered.

Caitlin felt overwhelmed at his hospitality. She hardly knew how to respond.

"It is a great pleasure," she said.

"And we thank you for your graciousness," Caleb said.

"Are you a king?" Scarlet stepped forward and asked. "Is there a real princess here?"

The king looked down and broke into uproarious laughter, louder and deeper than before. "Well now, I am a king, yes indeed—but there is no princess here I'm afraid. Just us men. But perhaps you shall rectify that, my beauty!" he said with a laugh, and took two steps forward, picked up Scarlet, and spun her around. "And what might your name be?"

Scarlet blushed, suddenly shy.

"Scarlet," she said, looking down. "And that's Ruth," she said, pointing down.

Ruth barked, as if in response, and McCleod set her down with a laugh, and stroked Ruth's fur.

"I'm sure you are all ravenous," he said. "To the castle!" he shouted. "It's time to celebrate!"

All his men shouted, turned as a group, and headed for the castle's entrance. As they did, rows of guards snapped to attention.

Sam draped an arm around Caitlin's shoulder, and Caleb around Polly's, as they all walked together towards the castle entrance. Caitlin knew she shouldn't, but despite herself, she allowed herself to hope that, once again, this time, they had found a permanent home, a place in the world that they could all, finally, be at peace in forever.

CHAPTER SIX

It was the warmest and most lavish welcome Caitlin could have imagined. Their arrival had been like one long celebration. They'd run into one coven member after another, and she saw faces she hadn't seen in what felt like forever— Barbara, Cain, and many others. They'd all sat for lunch at a huge banquet table, in the warm, stone castle, furs beneath their feet, torches along the walls, the fireplace roaring, and dogs running all around. The room felt warm and cozy, and Caitlin realized that it was cold outside—the end of October, Caitlin had been told. 1350. Caitlin couldn't believe it. She was nearly seven hundred years away from the 21st century.

She had always tried to imagine what life might be like in this time period, in the times of the knights, of armor, castles...but she had never imagined anything quite like this. Despite the stark change in surroundings, the lack of major towns or cities, the people were still very warm, very intelligent, very human. In many ways, not all that different from the people of her time.

Caitlin felt very at home in this time and place. She had spent hours catching up with Sam and Polly, hearing their stories, their version of what had happened to them back in England. She had been horrified to hear of what had happened between Sergei and Polly, and so proud of Sam for saving her.

And throughout the whole night, she couldn't help but notice that Sam barely took his eyes off of Polly. As a big sister, she sensed that a major shift had happened within him. He finally seemed more mature, and for the first time ever, truly and totally in love.

Yet Polly, this time, seemed a bit more evasive. It was harder for Caitlin to get an exact fix on where she stood, on her feelings for Sam. Maybe it was because Polly was more guarded. Or maybe it was because this time, Polly truly cared. Caitlin could sense, deep down, that Sam meant the world to her, and that she was being extra careful not to disclose her feelings, or mess it up. Caitlin did notice that every once in a while, when Sam looked away, Polly stole a quick glance back at him. But then she quickly averted her eyes, so that Sam wouldn't catch her looking.

Caitlin felt, beyond a doubt, that her brother and her best friend were about to become a couple. The idea of it thrilled her. And it amused her that both of them were still in denial of what was happening between them—and even trying to pretend that it wasn't.

The table was also filled with new human friends, and Caitlin met so many people who she felt close to. They were all warriors. The king sat at the head, surrounded by his dozens of knights. Throughout the afternoon, they all sang drinking songs, and laughed aloud as they recounted stories of battle, of hunting expeditions. Caitlin could tell that these Scottish people were warm, friendly, hospitable, loved to drink, and were great raconteurs. And yet they were also very noble and proud, and great warriors.

The meal and stories went on for hours, as lunch extended into late afternoon. Torches died out and were re-lit. Dozens of new logs were added to the massive, stone fireplace; huge vats of wine were replaced. Eventually, all the dogs tired out, feel asleep on the rugs. Scarlet finally feel asleep on Caitlin's lap, while Ruth curled up beside Scarlet. Ruth had been well-fed, thanks to Scarlet, who'd fed her a never-ending supply of meat. A dozen dogs were seated around the table, begging for scraps, but they all had the good sense to steer clear of Ruth. And Ruth, content, didn't seem interested in messing with them, either.

Some of the warriors, gutted from food and drink, eventually nodded off on their furs, too. Caitlin found herself drifting off, turning her mind to other times and places, other matters. She started to wonder what her next clue would be; if her Dad would be in this place and time; where her next journey would take her. Her eyes started to close, when suddenly, she heard her name.

It was the king, McCleod, addressing her over the din.

"And what do you think, Caitlin?" he asked again.

As he did, the jovial table slowly began to quiet, as people turned and looked her way.

Caitlin felt embarrassed, not having been listening to the conversation. The king looked at her, as if awaiting an answer. Finally, he cleared his throat.

"What do you think of the Holy Grail?" he asked again.

The Holy Grail? Caitlin wondered. *Was that what they had been talking about?*

She had no idea. She had not been thinking of the Holy Grail at all, and hardly even knew what it was. She wished now that she had been listening to their conversation. She tried to remember what it was, and thought back to childhood fairytales, to myths and legends. To the stories of King Arthur. Excalibur. The Holy Grail…

Slowly, it was coming back to her. If she recalled correctly, the Holy Grail was rumored to be a chalice or goblet, rumored to hold a special liquid….Yes, now it was coming back to her. Some people had said that the Holy Grail held the blood of Christ, that drinking it would make you immortal. If she remembered correctly, the knights had spent hundreds of years searching for it, had risked their lives trying to find it, to the ends of the earth. And no one ever had.

"Do you think it will ever be found?" McCleod asked again.

Caitlin cleared her throat, the entire table looking to her for an answer.

"Um…" she began, "I haven't really thought about it," she answered. "But if it really exists…then I don't see why it can't be found."

There was a small roar of approval at the table.

"You see," McCleod said to one of his knights. "She is an optimist. I, too, think it will be found."

"An old wives' tale," said a knight.

"And what will you do when you find it?" asked another knight. "That's the real question."

"Why, I shall make myself immortal," the king answered, breaking into a hearty laugh.

"You don't need the Holy Grail for that," said another knight. "All you need is to be turned."

A tense silence suddenly fell around the table. Clearly, this knight had overspoke, had crossed a line and mentioned something taboo. He lowered his head in shame, recognizing his mistake.

Caitlin saw McCleod's sudden, dark expression, and in that moment, she realized that he desperately wanted to be turned. And that he sorely resented Aiden's coven for not obliging him. Clearly, this knight had raised a sore point, the one point of tension between the two races.

"And what is it like?" the king asked aloud, directing his question to Caitlin, for some reason. "Immortality?"

Caitlin wondered why he'd had to ask her, of all the vampires in the room. Couldn't he have picked someone else?

She thought about that. *What was it like?* What could she possibly say? On the one hand, she loved immortality, loved living in all these times and places, seeing her family and friends again and again, in each new time and place. On the other hand, some parts of her still wished she had a normal, simple life, wished that there was a normal arc to things. Most of all, she found herself surprised at how brief immortality seemed: on the one hand, it felt like life forever—but on the other hand, it still always felt to her like there was never enough time.

"It doesn't feel as permanent as you might imagine."

The rest of the table nodded in approval at her response.

McCleod suddenly rose from his chair. As he did, all the others rose at attention.

Just as Caitlin was turning over the odd exchange in her head, wondering if she had upset him, she suddenly felt his presence behind her. She turned, and he was standing over her.

"You are wise beyond your years," he said. "Come with me. And bring your friends. I have something to show you. Something that has been waiting for you a very long time."

Caitlin was surprised. She had no idea what it might be.

McCleod turned and strutted out the hall, and Caitlin and Caleb rose, followed by Sam and Polly, and followed him. They looked at each other in wonder.

They crossed the large, stone floor, following the king through the enormous chamber and out a side door, as the knights around the table slowly sat back down and resumed their meal.

McCleod walked in silence, strutting down a narrow, torch-lit hall, with Caitlin, Caleb, Sam and Polly following. The ancient stone halls twisted and turned, leading them to a staircase.

McCleod took a torch off the wall and led the way down the darkened staircase, into seeming blackness. As they walked, Caitlin began to wonder where exactly, he was leading them. What could he possibly have to show them? An ancient weapon of some sort?

Finally, they reached a subterranean level, well lit by torches, and Caitlin was amazed at the sight. The low, arched ceiling glittered, plated in gold. Caitlin could see illustrated images of Christ, Knights, scenes from the Bible, mixed with various odd signs and symbols. The floor was an ancient, well-worn stone, and Caitlin couldn't help but feel as if they'd entered a secret treasure chamber.

Caitlin's heart began to beat faster, as she sensed something important awaiting them. She strutted faster, hurrying to catch up to the King.

"The treasury vault of the McCleod clan for a thousand years. It is down here where we hold our most sacred treasure, weapons and possessions. But there is one possession which is more valuable, more sacred, than all of them."

He stopped and turned to her.

"It is a treasure we have been saving just for you."

He turned and lifted a torch off a side wall, and as he did, a hidden door in the wall suddenly opened up in the stone. Caitlin was amazed: she would have had no idea it was there.

McCleod turned and led them down another twisting corridor. Finally, they came to a stop in a small alcove area. Before them was a throne, on which sat a lone object: a small, jeweled treasure chest. Torchlight flickered over it, illuminating it, and McCleod gingerly reached down and picked it up.

Slowly, he lifted the lid. Caitlin could not believe it.

There, inside the chest, sat a single piece of ancient parchment, a faded, antique color, wrinkled and torn in half. It was covered in ancient handwriting, in a delicate script, in a language Caitlin did not recognize. Along its edges were multi-colored letters, drawings and symbols, and in its center was a drawing, semi-circular. But given that it was torn in half, Caitlin could not make out what it was supposed to be.

"For you," he said, gingerly lifting it and holding it out to her.

Caitlin held the piece of torn parchment, feeling it crinkle in her hands, and held it up to the torchlight. It was a torn page, perhaps from a book. With all of its delicate symbology, it looked like a piece of art in its own right.

"It is the missing page to the Holy Book," McCleod explained. "When you find the book, that page will be complete. And when it is, you will find the relic we are all searching for."

He turned and faced her.

"The Holy Grail."

CHAPTER SEVEN

Caitlin sat in her large room in Dunvegan in Castle at a writing desk, looking out the window at the sunset sky. She examined the torn page McCleod had given her, holding it up to the light. She slowly ran her fingertips along the embossed, Latin letters. They looked and felt ancient. The entire page was so beautifully and intricately designed, and she marveled at the intricate colors along the paper's edges. Back then, she realized, books were made to be works of art in and of themselves.

Caleb lay on their bed, while Scarlet and Ruth were sprawled out on a pile of furs before the fireplace on the far side of the room. This room was so sprawling, that even with all of them in it, Caitlin still felt alone with her thoughts. In the adjacent room, she knew, were Sam and Polly. It had been a long day, and a long feast with Aiden's coven and the king's men, and they were all settling in for the night.

Caitlin could not stop thinking about the torn page, the clue, where it might lead her, and if it would yield the fourth key. Would her father be there this time? Could it be that he was waiting, close by? Her heart beat faster at the thought of it. Did that mean she would finally find the shield? That all of this would be over? And what would she do then? Where would she go next?

It was all too overwhelming for her to consider. She felt she just had to focus on the clue before her, to take it one step at a time. She thought of what McCleod had said about the holy Grail. He had told her that he and his men had devoted their lives to finding the grail. That legend had it that a woman would arrive and lead them to it. He believed that she, Caitlin, was that woman. Which was why he had given her his precious clue, the ancient piece of paper.

But Caitlin wasn't so sure. Was the grail just a myth? Or was it real? And how was it tied to her search?

Caitlin didn't know where all this lead, but as she reflected, she realized that, once again, she had finally found a place, in this castle, with these people, where she felt a sense of peace and comfort. She felt at home in Skye, in this castle, with this king, with his knights, and of course, being back with Aiden's coven again. She was thrilled to be reunited with Caleb,

Scarlet, Sam and Polly. Finally, once again, everything felt right in the world. It was cold and windy out there, and with a fire raging in her fireplace, she was cozy in here, and really didn't want to venture out there, hunting down more clues. She wanted to stay right here. She could see herself building a home here with Caleb, and Scarlet, and Ruth.

If they pressed on with their missions, how might that affect her relationship with Caleb? Or even endanger Scarlet or Ruth? It seemed that whenever she got close to finding another key, bad things started to happen.

Caitlin slowly set down the brittle piece of paper, and stared, instead, at her unopened journal before her, sitting on the desk. It was now worn, thick with use, looking like a relic in its own right. She reached out and slowly pulled back the pages, turning them all the way until she nearly reached the end of the book. She realized, with a start, that there weren't that many blank pages left. She couldn't believe it. When she'd first began this journal, it had seemed as if it would last forever.

She lifted the quill, blotted it into the ink, and began to scrawl.

I can't believe this journal is almost finished. I look back at some of my older entries, like the one from New

York City, and it feels like lifetimes ago. But it also feels like it all just happened yesterday.

I think back on all that I've been through, and I don't even know where to begin anymore. I feel like too much has gone by to catch you up on everything. So I will just fill you in on the most important things.

Caleb is alive. He survived his sickness. I'm back together with him now. And we are going to be married. Nothing makes me happier.

Scarlet, the most beautiful eight-year-old girl in the world, is in our lives. She is our daughter now. She survived her sickness, too, and I am overjoyed.

Not to mention Ruth, who has grown bigger and stronger than Rose ever was, and might just be the most loyal and protective animal I've ever seen. She's as much a part of our family as Scarlet and Caleb.

And I'm thrilled to be reunited with Sam and Polly. Finally, I feel like my whole family is back together again, under one roof.

I am nervous for our wedding. Caleb and I haven't had a chance to talk about it yet, but I feel it will be soon. When I was younger, I always tried to imagine my wedding day. But I never imagined anything remotely like what this might be. A vampire wedding? What will it look like?

I hope that he still loves me as much as I love him. I sense that he does. I wonder if he is nervous for the wedding, too?

I look down at my ring, at the ring he gave me, so beautiful, covered in all these shining jewels. It doesn't *feel real. Not any of it. But at the same time, I feel like I've been connected to him forever.*

I want to find my Dad. I really do. But I don't want to search anymore, and I don't want things to change. Any of this. I want to be with Caleb. And I want our wedding to happen. Is it wrong to put our wedding first?

Caitlin closed her journal and sent down the quill. Still lost in another world, she blinked and looked around the room. She wondered how much time had passed while she was reflecting; she looked out the window and saw that it was twilight, and as she glanced about the room, she saw that Scarlet and Ruth were still fast asleep. On the other side of the room, beneath the torchlight, Caleb seemed to be asleep, too.

Caitlin also found herself feeling sleepy. She felt she needed to clear her head, to get some air. She got up from the desk quietly and began to cross the room, determined to slip outside. She grabbed a fur shawl on the way, wrapping it around her shoulders. Just as she reached the door, though, she heard a soft clearing of the throat.

She looked over and saw Caleb looking at her, one eye open, beckoning her.

She turned and walked over to his side, and as he patted the bed, she sat beside him.

He smiled as he slowly opened his eyes. As always, she was struck by his beauty. His facial features were so perfect, so clean and smooth, his jaw line and cheekbone prominent, his lips full and smooth, his nose angular and perfect. He blinked with his long eyelashes, then slowly reached out and ran one hand through her hair.

"We've hardly had a chance to talk," he said.

"I know," she smiled back.

"I want you to know how much I still love you," he said.

Caitlin smiled. "I love you, too."

"And that I can't wait to be married to you," he added, his smile widening.

He sat up and kissed her, and they kissed for a long time beneath the torchlight.

Caitlin felt her heart warm. That was exactly what she had been wanting to hear. It was uncanny how he had always been able to read her thoughts.

"Now that we're here, I want to marry you. Before we continue on our search. Right here. In this place." He studied her. "What do you think?"

She looked back at him, her heart racing with conflicting emotions. It was exactly what she wanted, too. But she was also scared. She wasn't sure how to respond.

Finally, she stood.

"Where are you going?" he asked.

"I'll be back soon," she said. "I just need to clear my head."

She kissed him one last time, then turned and walked out the room, closing the door softly behind her. She knew that if she stayed, she would end up in his arms, in the bed. And she first really needed to gather her thoughts. Not that she had any doubts about him. Or about their marriage. Or about their wedding. But she still felt conflicted, divided, over whether she needed to be out there, pursuing her mission. Was it selfish to put the wedding first?

As Caitlin walked down the empty, stone corridor, her footsteps echoing, she spotted a stairwell heading up, and saw natural light filtering down it. The castle roof, she realized. That was just the place she could go to get privacy and fresh air.

Caitlin hurried up the steps and into the twilight air. It was colder up here than she imagined, a late October wind driving strong. She wrapped her furs tightly over her shoulders, and was grateful for the warmth.

As Caitlin walked slowly along the ramparts, she looked out over the countryside in what little light was left. It was breathtakingly beautiful. On one side, the castle was perched beside a vast and lake, covered in mist. On the other side was a great expanse of trees and hills and valleys. This place felt magical.

Caitlin walked to the edge of a rampart, staring out, taking in the landscape—when suddenly, she sensed another presence. She didn't know how that could be possible, as the entire roof had been empty. She slowly turned, not sure what to expect.

She couldn't believe it.

Standing there, at the far end of the roof, was a lone figure, his back to her, looking out over the lake. An electric thrill ran through her. She didn't need to see his long, flowing robes, his long silver hair, or the staff at his side to know who it was.

Aiden.

Could it really be? she wondered. Or was it just an illusion in the twilight?

She crossed the roof, slowly walking over to him, and stopped a few feet away. He stood so still, his hair blowing in the breeze, not turning. For a moment, she wondered if he was real. Then came his voice.

"You have come far," he said, his back still to her.

Slowly, he turned and faced her. His eyes were a large shining blue, even in the dim light, and they seemed to look right through her. As usual, his face was expressionless. Intense.

Caitlin was thrilled to see him here. There had been so many questions she was dying to ask him, and as usual, he seemed to show up at just the moment when she needed guidance the most.

"I didn't know if I would see you again," she said.

"You will always see me," he answered. "Sometimes in person, and sometimes otherwise," he answered cryptically.

A silence hung between them, as she tried to gather her thoughts.

"There is only key left," she found herself saying. "Does that mean I will see my father soon?"

He studied her, then slowly looked away.

Finally, he said, "That depends on your actions, doesn't it?"

His habit of answering a question with a question always drove her mad. She had to try again.

"The new clue," she said. "The page. The torn page. I don't know where it leads. I don't know what to look for. Or where."

Aiden stared off into the horizon.

"Sometimes clues look for you," he answered. "You know that now. Sometimes you must wait for things to be revealed."

Caitlin thought about that. Was he telling her to do nothing?

"Then…is there nothing for me to do?" she asked.

"There is much for you to do," Aiden responded.

He turned and faced her, and slowly, for the first time in as long as Caitlin could remember, he broke into a smile. "You have a wedding to plan."

Caitlin felt herself smiling back.

"I wanted to. But I was afraid that it was frivolous," she said. "That I should put on hold. That I should be searching first."

Aiden slowly shook his head.

"A vampire wedding is not frivolous. It is a sacred event. It is the merging of two vampire souls. It brings more power to each of you, and more power to our entire coven. And it will only deepen your growth, your skills. I am proud of you. You have grown greatly. But if you are to evolve to the next level, you need this. Each union brings its own power. Both for the couple, and for the individual."

Caitlin felt relieved, excited—but also nervous.

"But I don't know how to plan this kind of wedding. I would barely even know how to plan a human wedding."

Aiden smiled. "You have many friends who will help you. And I will preside over the ceremony." He smiled. "I am a priest, after all."

Caitlin smiled wide, liking the thought of that.

"So, what do I do now?" Caitlin asked, excited, nervous, not knowing where to begin.

He smiled.

"Go to Caleb. And say yes. Let love take care of the rest."

CHAPTER EIGHT

Kyle trekked through the bogs of southern Scotland, fuming with hatred. With every step he took, he raged at the thought of Caitlin, running free, eluding him, in time after time, place after place. He dwelled on ways he could capture and kill her, exact revenge.

He had already exhausted nearly every method he could think, and she always seemed to slip through his grasp. He did manage to exact a small, petty revenge in poisoning her family. He smiled inwardly at the thought of that.

But it wasn't enough. This had gone on already way too long, and the last time they'd met, he had to admit it, she had overpowered him. He was shocked at her strength, her fighting skills. She had actually outfought him. It was beyond anything he could have anticipated.

A part of him had feared this, which was why he had gone to such lengths to poison her, to avoid a head-on confrontation. But that, too, had backfired. He'd poisoned Caleb by accident, and while he felt certain that his poison had killed Caleb, he hadn't had a chance to confirm it, as he'd had to flee in the night.

This was the last time and place, Kyle vowed to himself, that this would happen, that he would pursue her. Either he would kill her for sure this time, or he would die trying. There was no retreat, no surrender. No more times or places. This would be his last and final stand. Here, in Scotland.

And for this final stand, he had a grand strategy, the grandest of them all. The vampire poison had seemed a good idea at the time, but in retrospect, it was just too risky, left too much room for chance. His new idea, though, could not possibly fail.

In coming up with this new scheme, Kyle had thought back to all the times and places he had cornered in Caitlin, and tried to recall the time he had come closest to killing her. He concluded that it was back in New York, when he'd captured her brother, Sam, had him under his control, and used him to shapeshift and trick Caitlin. That had nearly worked.

Shapeshifting, Kyle realized, was the key. With this type of trickery, he could dupe Caitlin, gain her confidence, and then kill her for good.

But the problem was, Kyle did not possess this skill. He did, though, knew one person, in this time and place, who did.

His old protégé.

Rynd.

Centuries before, Kyle had trained a fleet of the most vicious, sadistic vampires who'd ever roamed the face of the earth. Rynd had been one of his shining stars. He'd become too vicious even for Kyle to handle, and Kyle eventually had to expel him.

Last Kyle heard, Rynd was living in this time and place, hiding out in the remote Southern corner of Scotland. Kyle would find him now. After all, Kyle had taught him everything he knew, and he figured Rynd owed him one. It was the least he could do for his old mentor. All Kyle needed from him was for him to summon his old shapeshifting trick, just once.

Kyle, ankle deep in mud, smiled at the thought of it. Yes, Rynd was exactly what he needed to dupe Caitlin, to finish her off for good. This time, it was a plan that could not fail.

Kyle looked up, taking in the scene. It was cold, and windy, and the dampness in the air seeped into his bones. It was twilight, his favorite time of day, and there was a heavy fog creeping over the ancient wood. It was just his kind of day. If there was anything Kyle loved more than twilight, it was fog. Kyle felt positively at home.

Suddenly, his senses were on high alert. A creepy feeling raised the hair on his skin, and something told him that Rynd was close.

As Kyle walked into the fog, he heard a slight creaking, and looked up and spotted something moving. As the fog parted, Kyle could make out a barren forest of dead trees, and as he looked closer, he saw objects hanging from the branches.

As he stepped forward and examined them, he realized they were bodies—humans—dead, hanging upside down by their feet, tied by rope to the branches. They swung slowly in the wind, and the sound of rope creaking on wood permeated the air. From the look of these corpses, it seemed they had been killed long ago; their skin was blue, there were telltale holes in their necks, and Kyle realized they had been fed upon, drained of blood.

Rynd's work.

As the fog continued to part, Kyle spotted hundreds—no thousands—of bodies, all hanging. It was obvious that they'd all been kept alive for some time, tortured slowly for days. It was sadistic, malicious stuff.

Kyle admired it. It was something he himself would have done in his heyday.

Kyle knew that Rynd had to be very, very close.

Suddenly, out of the mist, there appeared a solitary figure, slowly approaching. Kyle squinted into the fog, trying to make out who it was.

And when he realized, his heart stopped.

It couldn't be.

Standing there, before him, was his mother. His *real* mother, his human mother, before he was ever turned. It was the one person he loved most in the world, the one person who could recall what a kind person he had been before he'd been turned—and the one person who reminded him of his own humanity.

Kyle felt as if he'd been struck through the heart. Pangs of guilt and remorse tore him apart.

At the sight of her, he dropped to his knees, and wept.

"Mother!" Kyle yelled, weeping like a child.

She came closer to him, arms outstretched, a compassionate smile on her face.

Kyle could not comprehend what she was doing in this time and place. Had she come to ask him to repent?

"Come to me, my child," she said, beckoning him.

Kyle rose to his feet, and took a step forward to her.

The second he did, he regretted it.

Suddenly, he felt his whole world turn upside down, as he went rocketing upwards into the air. This was followed by a loud creaking noise, and as Kyle swung side to side, staring down at the ground, he realized he'd stepped into a trap.

The silver rope had tightened around his feet, had propelled him high into the air, twenty feet off the ground, dangling upside down. Kyle reached up to tear it off, but realized it was vampire-resistant material, one he could not tamper with.

He hung there, swinging upside down, infuriated. He was infuriated at being caught, and infuriated by his own stupidity. More than anything, he was infuriated that he had been tricked.

An evil laugh sounded in the distance.

Kyle recognized that laugh anywhere, as a chill ran up his spine. Rynd.

"So, the master comes home to roost," Rynd growled, in his deep, gravelly voice.

Into Kyle's line of vision, upside down, came an imposing vampire, flanked by dozens of other vampires. He was bigger and meaner and uglier than Kyle had ever remembered. He must have been a foot taller than Kyle, with huge, black empty eyes, gleaming fangs, and a square, pockmarked face. He wore his thick black hair straight back on his head, braided tightly.

"You bastard," Kyle spat. "You shapeshifted into my mother."

"Oldest trick in the book," Rynd spat. "Who doesn't like his mother? Even a creature like you was bound to fall for it."

"You'll pay for that," Kyle snarled, embarrassed.

Rynd laughed.

"You stupid old bastard. Clearly, the only one who will pay now is you. Did you come to say your goodbyes for good, before I kill you?"

"I've come to order you to do me a favor," Kyle said.

Rynd laughed uproariously.

"Order me? You?"

He laughed again.

"I? Do *you* a favor?" he continued "The only favor I will do you is to put you far beneath the earth."

This was not going as Kyle had hoped. He knew it was time to try a different track.

"I have something that can help you," Kyle said.

"Nothing of yours can help me," Rynd snapped, and his eyes suddenly glowered in fury. "I'm beyond being helped by you or anyone or anything. I'm much stronger than you now."

"Set me down, and we can talk," Kyle said.

"It's too late for that," Rynd said. "If I set you down, it will be only to lie with the worms."

Kyle's heart stopped, as he heard the sickening sound of a silver sword being extracted from its scabbard. He watched as Rynd took several steps forward and raised it high. He began to swing, aiming for Kyle's throat, and Kyle could see from the look in his eyes, that it was a look meant to kill.

And Kyle suddenly realized that these moments might just be his last.

CHAPTER NINE

The day broke brisk and cold, and Caitlin woke up excited. Aiden had told her that the wedding preparations would begin immediately, on this day. She had woken Caleb when she'd returned and told him she'd be thrilled to marry him right away, and he'd been ecstatic. She'd slept the whole night in his arms, eager for dawn to break so that the preparations could begin.

Aiden had told her that the traditional vampire wedding was preceded by a day of tournaments, of jousting and sparring to test each other's skills. She was so curious to learn more about all the vampire rituals surrounding a wedding, and excited to begin the first step towards actually getting married. It still felt surreal to her.

As Caitlin walked out the castle, dressed in her sparring gear, she held Caleb's hand as they crossed the expansive castle grounds in the cold October morning, Scarlet and Ruth right behind them. In the distance, Caitlin could see the entire coven was already out and waiting—

dozens of Aiden's vampires, mixed with dozens of McCleod's human warriors. Standing among them were also Sam and Polly, beaming as they watched them approach. There must have been a hundred warriors in total, forming a large rectangle on the tournament field, all dressed in full battle gear, standing quietly, waiting.

Clearly, Caitlin and Caleb were the guests of honor today. Two warriors sounded a trumpet at their arrival, and the crowd parted ways as they walked through, and were prompted into the center of the open field. As Caitlin and Caleb stood there, Aiden slowly stepped forward and faced them. The crowd remained silent in the early morning, the only noise the slight rustling of the wind, and the flapping of banners.

"No vampire wedding may begin without a full day of tournaments. It is an ancient ritual. The tournaments are our way of keeping in mind that a vampire union is a union based on blood. Husband and wife are also a warrior team. Which is why we begin our day with you two fighting together. You will fight as a team, back to back. Against you will be pitted our best warriors. Together, you must protect each other, and fight your way through."

Aiden stepped back out of the circle, and slowly nodded to his men.

Caitlin stood in the center of the circle, back to back with Caleb, and felt a nervous rush as they were each suddenly thrown weapons. She caught hers in midair: wooden swords. She was relieved that they wouldn't be using live, deadly weapons; she wasn't worried about her own fighting skills, or Caleb's, but she was worried about hurting someone else.

There was little time to think. Within moments, they were charged by a dozen vampire and human warriors, coming at them from every direction. They, too, wielded wooden weapons—spears, swords, shields, lances, and other weapons she couldn't recognize at first. She felt Caleb's back flush up against hers, felt his muscles tense up, and felt reassured to have him at her side.

Within moments, the first attackers were in her face, swinging, slashing.

Caitlin's instincts took over. Her vampire speed and reflexes, all her years of training with Aiden, took. She found herself parrying and slashing back, kicking and dodging and rolling. As three vampires charged and brought down their swords at the same time in a well-coordinated attack, she spun and slashed all three swords away as she came back around, and kicked one hard with a spinning roundhouse kick, knocking him hard into the other warriors—who all landed on top of each other.

Caitlin looked up to see another warrior—this one a human—charging her with a large, wooden battle ax. He brought it down with two hands, aiming straight for her head, and she could tell that if he'd hit, the blow would really hurt. She was surprised at these human warriors' speed; if she hadn't been looking, he would have caught her.

But Caitlin's reflexes again kicked in, and she dodged out of the way at the last second, the wood whistling by her ear. As the warrior rushed past her, she leaned back and kicked him hard in the ribs, sending him to the ground.

Caitlin turned just in time to see a long wooden chain and mace being swung right for her chest. She jumped back, and it missed by a hair, as it grazed the tip of her clothing. She imagined what that mace would have done to her—even though it was wood. The warrior swung again, and this time, she could see he was aiming for Caleb.

Caleb, his back to her, had his hands full, slashing and parrying with two vampires and one human warrior. He didn't see the mace being swung right for him. The mace was coming down hard, and it was about to strike a hard blow on his shoulder.

Caitlin reached her sword high in the air and intercepting it before it reached Caleb. The chain, instead, wrapped several times around her sword, entangled in it. She then yanked it hard, and as she did, the warrior was pulled close to her; she then leaned back and sidekicked him hard in the gut, knocking the wind out of him.

Caitlin turned and leapt into the air, somersaulting over Caleb, and landing a double front kick on the chest of his opponent. She then reached down and grabbed his sword, swung around, and cracked one of Caleb's other opponents hard behind his knees, buckling him to the floor. Caleb followed up by kicking him in the chest, and sending him to the ground. The third warrior swung around and was about to crack Caitlin hard in the back with his wooden sword. She had made a stupid mistake—she had been too preoccupied with Caleb's other two warriors, and now she braced herself for a blow.

But at the last second, she heard the sound of wood on wood, and spun to see that Caleb had blocked the blow for her, then reached over and kicked him, knocking him to the ground.

Caitlin looked at Caleb with gratitude, and he exchanged the same grateful look. She could really feel that they were in this together.

Dozens more warriors prepared to charge, but suddenly there was the blow of a loud whistle, and everyone stopped.

Aiden stepped forward.

"Well done," he said, as Caitlin and Caleb stood there, out of breath. "Now, we switch to jousting."

The warriors immediately repositioned themselves, as servants brought out horses from the castle grounds. These horses were beautifully bedecked, covered in jewels, and the kings' men, wearing chainmail, handed out several shining lances.

Caitlin found herself led to a horse, which she mounted, then found herself handed a huge lance.

On the far side of the field, facing her, a vampire warrior mounted a horse and scowled back at her. She recognized him immediately. Cain.

Another whistle sounded, and Caitlin's horse charged forward at a gallop. The warriors all cheered, as the two galloped right for each other. Caitlin could feel the wind in her hair, out of breath at the speed of the horse, doing her best to wield the heavy lance. She saw the expression in Cain's face, bearing down on her, and tried instead to focus not on his eyes, but on his chest. On where to place the lance. He was taller than her, and had the advantage. But she decided not to rely on her senses.

Caitlin closed her eyes, and tuned in. She sensed the spirit of the horse, felt its minute movements, its breathing; she sensed her opponent's horse, her opponent's weaknesses. She felt every muscle in the horse as they ran, felt the indents in the terrain, the cool feel of her lance's hilt. When she opened her eyes again, she was but feet away—and she let her arm guide the lance to its proper place.

It was a direct hit. She hit Cain on his rib cage, a split-second before he reached her. Cain fell off his horse, tumbling to the ground hard, and the crowd cheered.

Caitlin jousted again and again, for what felt like hours, against vampire warriors, against human warriors....Time and again, she was victorious.

Simultaneously, several more jousting lanes were opened and more horses were brought out, so that Caleb was jousting other opponents beside her, and others were jousting beside him. It became a jovial atmosphere, as dozens of horses were charging each other at any given time, the air filled with the sound of clanging. The royal musicians came out and played on their trumpets and lutes, adding a festive, medieval flare to the festival. Eventually vats of wine were also rolled out, along with vats of blood, and people drank freely throughout the day.

As Caitlin took a break at one point, she noticed that her brother Sam was up on a horse, jousting opponents. He knocked one off easily, looking graceful as he did. She marveled at how far he had come.

She noticed that Polly was jousting, too. After defeating one opponent, she came around, and found herself pared off with Sam.

Caitlin could see the look of anxiety in Sam's eyes: it was clear he did not want to fight her.

But they were pitted against each other, and as the crowd screamed out, they had no choice but to gallop towards one another. At the last second, Sam raised his lance just enough to miss her, allowing her to strike him square in the chest. Caitlin watched as, for the first time that day, Sam fell from his horse, hitting the ground hard. She then noticed the confused and surprised expression on Polly's face. Clearly, Sam had taken a fall for her.

As the day grew long, the jousting eventually subsided, and was replaced with other contests and games. There were games of throwing small metal balls into circular targets; games of lifting heavy boulders and throwing them; games with slingshots, with bows and arrows, and even games with spears, aiming for fish in a flowing creek.

Scarlet came running up to Caitlin when they took out the bows and arrows. "Please, Mommy, can I try?" she pleaded.

Caleb looked down at her. "I don't see why not."

Scarlet ran off with a delighted squeal, Ruth following. She grabbed the bows and arrows and took aim, with all the other warriors, at distant targets.

An amazed crowd began to gather around the girl, as one by one, warriors stopped what they were doing and stared. Caitlin, too was in shock. Scarlet hit every target perfectly, putting the grown warriors to shame. Caitlin couldn't believe it. Clearly, Scarlet had an innate skill. Caitlin wondered where it came from, and she felt more proud of her than ever.

As a never-ending stream of games and competitions came and went, the day grew more and more festive. Competitions started to peter out, replaced with banter, laughter and camaraderie, as more food and wine and blood were rolled out into the fields. As the sun slowly began to set, painting the sky in a blanket of orange, it transitioned to a full-fledged party, the day's former opponents all hugging each other, sharing drinks and huge pieces of meat over roasting fires. The tournaments transitioned to a feast.

Caitlin found Caleb, and the two shared drinks and food, laughing with human and vampire opponents they had fought on the field, surrounded by dozens of well-wishers, as torches were lit, the music grew louder, and the feast seemed to grow bigger and bigger. Caitlin fell her heart warm, surrounded by so many people she loved. It had not only been a fun day, but also a productive one, sharpening her skills in many ways, and teaching her much about Scarlet, too. It had also brought her and Caleb so much closer. She felt his love for her, and she felt the same. She was excited to think that the first step to their wedding day was now behind them, and that now they were that much closer to being wed.

"Now it's time to plan the wedding!" she yelled out excitedly, and a chorus of girls cheered their approval.

"It's going to be the most beautiful wedding you've ever seen," Polly said.

"I already have ideas about the flowers," Taylor chimed in.

Caitlin felt a bit overwhelmed, as all the girls suddenly began to chime in with their opinions. Before she could respond, she noticed something in the distance, over their shoulders, that made her stop in her tracks.

At first she thought she was seeing things, that it was an apparition. But then, as she watched, she saw it was real.

She felt the glass goblet slip from her fingers and crash to the ground, as she stood there, frozen, not believing what she saw.

There, in the distance, standing at the edge of the wood, watching her with his intense eyes, was a man she could never forget.

It was Blake.

CHAPTER TEN

Sam hadn't felt this happy in years. He'd a fun day of jousting with everyone, of joining in all the festivities surrounding Caitlin and Caleb's tournament day. He also, he had to admit, felt thrilled to be near Polly. In truth, he hadn't been able to stop thinking about her. He wondered if she realized he'd taken a fall for her on the jousting field. Fate had them paired against each other, and he knew there was little else he could do: in a million years, he would never lay a finger on her.

As they had rolled out vats of wine and of blood-infused alcohol, brought out huge slabs of meat roasting on a spit, Sam drank and ate and joined in the merriment. But he also kept finding himself looking for Polly. He spotted her hovering around Caitlin, already exuberant in her role as Maid of Honor, even more excited than usual as she discussed wedding preparations. Sam had kept waiting for an opportunity to take her aside, but none seemed to present itself.

It was a rowdy and bustling crowd of hundreds of vampires and human warriors, and as the drinking and feasting went on, the merriment turned into an outright dancing party. More musicians came, the music grew louder, the drink stronger, and people paired up, dancing in old-fashioned ways, locking arms and spinning in one circle, then locking arms and spinning in another. Men grabbed each other by the shoulder, forming circles, spinning round and round, and women grabbed women. Then they all switched off, and men and women danced with each other. There were smaller circles and bigger circles, couples breaking off and dancing with each other...It was spontaneous and chaotic, and Sam had never had so much fun.

Sam went from dancing in a circle of twelve men, to dancing in a circle of eight men and women, to locking arms with a human warrior he didn't know and spinning as fast as he could in one direction, then another. Partners were handed off to other partners, and Sam found himself dancing with nearly everyone in the field. At one point, he locked arms with Caitlin, and they danced in a circle, and both looked up, and laughed to see that they were dancing with each other. Sam was delighted to see her so happy. After that, he had danced with Caleb, and he'd felt happy, once again, that this would be his brother-in-law.

After several more dances, Sam found himself handed off and locking arms with someone else. The second he locked arms, Sam felt an electric thrill run through his body, and he did not need to look up to see who it was. Every pore in his body told him.

Polly.

Sam was almost nervous to look up and meet her eyes. He did slowly, and saw the most beautiful pair of blue eyes smiling back at him.

They spun around and around, first in one direction, then another, the music louder and louder. But instead of letting go, and switching to a new partner, as he had done every few seconds throughout the day, he held onto her. He found that she held onto him, too. Despite all the people trying to cut in, neither of them changed partners, for several minutes, until the song finally ended.

There was a lull in the music, and as the crowd cheered, the two of them stood there, staring at each other. Sam found his eyes locked with hers, and neither of them seemed willing to look away. Slowly, their smiles dropped, as their looks became more serious.

Sam felt he couldn't let her drift off into the crowd and dance with someone else. He needed to be with her. To talk to her. He wasn't sure exactly what he would say, but he did know that he didn't want to be without her at his side.

As she stood there, looking at him, Sam fumbled for words. He knew that he wanted to take her away from here, from this boisterous crowd. To be alone with her. But he didn't quite know what to say. He found himself nervous to ask her. What if she said no?

"Um…" Sam began, "do you think—do you—I mean—want to—I mean…"

Sam looked down, embarrassed. Finally, he summoned the courage and looked back up.

Polly was looking at him with a confused expression, waiting.

"Would you like to take a walk with me?" Sam asked, feeling his cheeks blushing.

Polly slowly smiled, raising an eyebrow.

"Do you mean just the two of us? Alone?" she asked, playfully.

Sam felt his heart pounding. It was strange, but he felt as if he were meeting Polly for the first time. And he didn't understand her hesitation. Was she just being playful? Or was she not interested?

"I mean—um—only if you want—I don't want to—um—interrupt you or anything—"

Polly smiled.

"Of course, I would love to," she said.

Sam broke into a smile, incredibly relieved. He held out an arm, and as she linked arms with him, the two of them walked off, through the crowd. The music was starting up again, and the others were beginning a new dance.

But Sam barely heard the music, and he clutched her tightly as they walked through the crowd and into the open field, he hoped that nothing would get between them again.

*

Sam was awestruck at the landscape as he walked with Polly, holding hands, into the sunset. He saw the horizon aglow in shades of red and purple, and he thought once again that this island was the most beautiful place he'd ever been. Before him stretched a vista of mountains, valleys, hills, and in the far distance, he could see the great open expanse that was the ocean. The hills were covered in a rich, vibrant green moss, and as they walked in the soft grass, they passed a roaring creek, and a small waterfall. He felt as if he were standing in the very place where Earth was created.

The two of them strolled at a casual pace, and while many minutes had passed since they'd left the party, neither of them had spoken a word. It was partly because the scene was breathtaking, but also, Sam realized, because he found himself nervous, tongue-tied. And he could sense that Polly was, too.

He wasn't sure exactly what it was he wanted to say to her. He just wanted to be with her, to spend time with her, to be alone with her. He guessed that what he had to say, to express, was non-verbal.

Sam didn't quite understand the strong feelings that were taking over him for Polly. He hadn't felt this way about her when they'd first met, and he'd never felt this way for any other girl before. He'd been attracted to other girls before, but with Polly, it was different: it was deeper than mere attraction. He didn't quite understand what was happening to him, or how it all happened so quickly. It seemed like only yesterday that he didn't think he was interested in Polly at all, and that he was convinced that she wasn't interested in him, either.

But since landing back in this time and place, he finally realized how much she meant to him. Still, he didn't quite know how to express it. He didn't want to scare her away, and he was nervous to say anything, in case she didn't feel the same way about him.

"Sorry to take you away from the party," Sam said, not knowing what else to say.

Polly gave him a funny look, and he immediately regretted his choice of words. It was not at all what he'd meant to say.

"Why are you sorry?" Polly asked. "I'm not sorry."

"Um…I mean…" Sam began, "…I mean, like, I didn't mean to interrupt things."

"So then why did you invite me out?" Polly asked.

"No reason," Sam said quickly, and regretted it again.

He didn't seem able to stop himself from saying the wrong thing, and his momentum seemed to carry him. "Just to get some fresh air, I guess."

Polly gave him another funny look, and he regretted it even more. Why couldn't he just come out and say what was on his mind? He knew that vampires could read minds, and in this case, he really wished that Polly would just read his, and make it easier on him. But it seemed that she wasn't trying to, or didn't want to.

"Oh," Polly said. "I thought that, maybe, it was something more than that."

"Like what?" Sam asked.

Now he was really kicking himself. *You are such an idiot*, he thought to himself. He had wanted to say: *yes, it was something else. I brought you here to tell you how I feel about you.* But he didn't seem to be able to summon the courage.

Polly, looking disappointed, shrugged, and the two of them continued to walk, up and down the mossy hills, in silence.

Having messed it up so much, Sam now really had no idea what to say to break the silence. He was furious with himself for not having the courage to express what was on his mind.

Thankfully, the terrain changed. They walked up a small hill, and suddenly, before them, was the most breathtaking view he'd ever seen: down below, hundreds of feet, was the ocean, lit up in every shade of red and orange and purple he could imagine. They stood at the edge of a cliff, and from where they were, it seemed as if they were looking out at the entire universe.

"Wow," Sam whispered.

Sam couldn't take his eyes off the view. That is, until he caught the reflection in Polly's eyes. He found himself turning and staring at her, instead.

Polly must have sensed his staring, because she eventually turned and looked back at him.

Their eyes locked.

Sam could feel his breath shortening, his heartbeat racing. He had no idea what to say from here. He found it relatively easy to interact with girls when he didn't care as much. But he'd never found himself caring for someone as much as this.

Sam couldn't understand it. Polly had always been so talkative; in fact, he could barely remember a time when she hadn't filled the air with conversation. Now, on this painfully quiet walk, she had barely said a word. Why now, of all times, when he needed her to talk the most?

Finally, thankfully, Polly broke the silence.

"Why did you take the fall for me in our joust?" Polly asked softly, staring into his eyes.

Sam swallowed, not sure how to respond. He was determined, this time, not to mess it up.

"Because I could never hurt you," he said. Then, feeling a burst of courage, he added, "I would always take the fall for you."

Sam was proud of himself, and expected that Polly would finally understand how much he cared for her.

But to his surprise, instead, her brow furrowed in consternation.

"I don't need you, or anyone else, to take the fall for me," she snapped, clearly offended. "I'm a perfectly good fighter in my own right. I'd rather lose because I lost then lose because someone threw a match for me."

Sam didn't know what to say. This was not how he had pictured this going at all. He'd thought she'd be grateful that he took the fall, and couldn't understand why she was so upset.

"Um…" he began, "I wasn't trying to upset you."

"Then why did you do it?" she answered, more firmly, her brow still creased.

Sam had no choice. He knew that it was now or never.

"Because I love you," he heard himself saying, flatly.

It was a surreal moment, as if someone else were there, saying the words, planting them in his mouth. He could not believe that he'd somehow summoned the courage to say it.

Polly stared at him, seeming surprised, too, and slowly, her facial expression shifted from anger to disbelief. For the first time, Polly seemed speechless.

Sam's heart was pounding in his chest, and he could barely breathe. But at least he had done it. Now, if she didn't feel the same, she could walk away. Sam half-expected her to respond that she liked him as a friend, but didn't feel the same way about him, and then turn and walk away. He braced himself.

But, to his surprise, she stood in place, and stared back. He wished that now, more than ever, he could read her mind. But vampire mind-reading always seemed off limits when it came to matters of love. Sam knew that it was now or never.

As the sun broke through a dark patch in the clouds, lighting up the entire horizon, slowly lighting her face and glowing blue eyes, Sam stepped forward, leaned in and brought his lips to hers.

Her lips were the softest thing he had ever felt.

But at first, they didn't kiss him back. He waited a moment, hoping that she would kiss him back, hoping he hadn't made a fool of himself.

And then, a second later, she did.

And as she did, he felt his entire world melting into hers. And he knew that, finally, he had found true love.

CHAPTER ELEVEN

Caitlin found herself walking, in the twilight, by herself, as the mist spread over the Isle of Skye. Her party long ended, she'd felt the need to take a long walk, to clear her head. As she walked, she looked down, and saw the mossy terrain, and noticed her bare feet were sinking into it, and she wondered why she hadn't worn shoes.

She looked up, and found herself crossing a small, arched footbridge, and as she looked over the edge, she saw a drop of hundreds of feet, down into the raging ocean. She somehow knew that if she slipped off this bridge, even an inch, her life would be over.

She crossed the bridge, which seemed to take forever, and as she reached the other side, she looked up, and through the mist, there came into view an enormous castle—the largest and most fantastical castle she had ever seen, replete with arches and spires in every direction, and encircled by a moat. As she approached, slowly, the drawbridge lowered, creaking, and then landed with a slam.

She continued walking, onto the heavy oak of the bridge, and suddenly, there was a lone figure in the entrance, appearing out of the mist.

She felt her heart stop.

Blake.

Caitlin stopped in her tracks, her heart pounding, and as she did, he walked out to her. He reached out and took her hand, and accompanied her, leading her towards the entrance.

She knew, she just knew, that this was his castle.

A part of her wanted to turn and run; but she was helpless. She let him lead her, through the entrance, and as he did, the drawbridge slammed shut behind them, locking them in.

The castle was cavernous and dim, lit only by sporadic torchlight. She found herself being led up a marble, winding staircase, up and up, past an endless number of floors. He then led her down corridor after corridor, until finally, they reached a massive, arched door. She knew this was his room.

He reached up and opened the door and Caitlin, thinking of Caleb, wondering where he was, wanted to turn and run.

But as Blake took her hand, she found herself helpless to resist.

He picked her up and carried her in his arms into the room. His brown eyes blazed with the intensity that she remembered.

Slowly, gently, he laid her down on the biggest bed she had ever seen, onto the softest linens and pillows she had ever felt. He sat beside her, then leaned down, and gently kissed her on the lips.

Despite herself, she was helpless to resist.

Suddenly, there was a pounding on the door, a metal knocker slamming into the oak.

Caitlin's heart stopped, as she knew that it was Caleb, coming to check on her.

"Caitlin!" screamed the voice from behind the door.

Caitlin tried to get up, but Blake held her in place. He lifted a single finger and placed it on her lips.

"Shhh," he said.

The door banged again. "Caitlin!"

"Caitlin!" came a voice.

Caitlin woke with a start, sitting straight up in bed and breathing hard. Disoriented, she tried to figure out where she was.

She looked around and realized she was awake, in her room, in Dunvegan Castle, and that she lay alone in bed. She saw Scarlet lying on her daybed, Ruth in her arms, on the far side of the room. She looked out the window and saw the sun rising, the day beginning to break.

She wasn't in Blake's castle; she wasn't anywhere near Blake. It had all just been a dream. A terrifying dream. She felt a wave of relief; and yet, at the same time, it had felt so real. Even though it was just a dream, she felt terribly guilty, as if she had cheated on Caleb. She had to forcibly remind herself that it was just a dream. She had done nothing wrong.

She looked over at her empty bed, looked around the room and saw no sign of Caleb. Where was he?

Then she remembered. As part of the vampire wedding ritual, the bride and groom were supposed to sleep apart during the days leading up to the wedding.

The door banged again.

"Caitlin!" yelled an excited female voice.

Caitlin got up, put on a silk robe, and hurried for the door.

Ever since she had seen Blake at the festivities, it had been hard for her to get him out of her head. And that upset her. She loved Caleb now, and Caleb only. Yet still, Blake haunted the periphery of her consciousness. She wished she could erase him completely from her memory, out of loyalty to Caleb, but she just couldn't.

After she had spotted him, and he had disappeared again, she'd asked the others about him, and was shocked to discover that Blake lived there, with the coven. Caitlin hadn't expected that. The idea had never even crossed her mind—especially since she had not seen him with the others upon first entering Skye.

As Caitlin crossed the room and opened the double doors, still nervous, she half-expected to see Blake standing there, despite the female voice.

But luckily, it was Polly. She stood there excitedly, with a big smile on her face. She looked happier and more content than Caitlin had ever seen her.

"Will you get up already?" Polly exclaimed, strutting past her into the room. "We're going to be late!"

As Caitlin took a deep breath, closed the doors, and followed Polly into her own room, she was beginning to feel relieved again. Polly always had a way of distracting her from her troubles.

"Late for what?" Caitlin asked, confused.

"Just for preparations for the biggest day of your life!" Polly said, exasperated. "It's the final day before your wedding! Today, we need to prepare everything for the big ceremony. The flowers, your dress, the feast, the ceremony—"

Caitlin held up a hand, already overwhelmed. She could tell that Polly was in her element, as if she'd been anticipating this forever. But this was hardly Caitlin's expertise. All these preparations overwhelmed her; she just wanted to be married to Caleb. She didn't feel the need for any of this pomp. And even if she did, it was certainly too early in the morning to process all of this.

"I'm hardly even awake, Polly," Caitlin protested.

Polly smiled and strutted across the room and began picking an outfit for Caitlin, throwing clothes off a dresser and onto Caitlin's bed.

"That's what I'm here for," Polly said.

Caitlin could see that she was determined, more excited than she'd ever seen her. She could also detect something else in her friend: a sense of peace, of contentment, one that she had never quite seen. Something had shifted within Polly: if Caitlin was not mistaken, it seemed as if she were in love.

Caitlin immediately thought of Sam. The last she'd seen the two of them, they were walking away from the party, hand-in-hand. Had something happened?

Caitlin examined Polly as she hurried over to her and excitedly draped a shawl over Caitlin's shoulders.

"Polly?" Caitlin asked, smiling.

Polly finally turned and looked at her.

"I sense something different about you," she said.

Caitlin noticed the slightest bit of red in Polly's cheeks. Yes, she was definitely blushing.

"Nothing's different," Polly answered.

But Caitlin already saw what she needed to see. Sam and Polly were officially together.

The thought of it made Caitlin happy. There was nothing she'd like more than for Polly to be part of her family. Her sister. Her *real* sister.

Suddenly, the door slammed open, and in marched Taylor, Barbara, and several other girls from Aiden's coven. They were all flushed, as happy and excited as Polly, dressed in fineries, carrying flowers. They cheered as they entered. They gathered around Caitlin, practically buzzing with excitement.

Caitlin was taken aback.

"It's not my wedding day yet!" she protested.

"No," Taylor said. "But it's only a day away! And today's your preparation day. There's so much for us to do. It's so exciting!"

Ruth barked, and Caitlin looked over and saw Scarlet standing beside her, tugging on her robe, looking up in excitement.

"Can I help, too?" she asked. "Please, mommy, you promised! You said I could be the flower girl! I want to help! With everything! This is my first wedding, after all!"

The girls all broke into laughter, as Caitlin reached down and hugged Scarlet.

"Of course you can, sweetheart," Caitlin said.

Caitlin turned to the others. "What about Caleb?" she asked. "Won't he help plan, too?"

"Not today," Polly said. "Today is the girls' day. And to begin, I have a surprise for you."

The other girls quieted in anticipation, and Caitlin could tell they were all in on some secret. Caitlin watched with curiosity as Polly strutted across the room, followed by the others, and approached a knob lodged in the wall which Caitlin hadn't noticed before. Polly pulled it and revealed a large closet, recessed into the wall.

And there, sitting alone inside, was a sight that made Caitlin's heart drop.

Sitting in the huge closet, hanging by itself, was the most beautiful wedding dress Caitlin had ever seen. It was endlessly long, made of lace, with a narrow, bejeweled belt around the waist. It had long sleeves, and fanned out at the waist, with a train that seemed to go on forever. Surprisingly, it had dramatic, high collars, framing the neck.

And most surprising of all, it was black.

Polly reached in and removed the dress. Two of the girls hurried over and helped, holding its train so that it wouldn't touch the floor.

Caitlin was so overcome by this surprise, by the beauty of the dress, by the thoughtfulness of Polly and all these girls, she didn't know what to say. She wanted to thank them, to gush over it, but she found herself speechless.

"It's black," Caitlin heard herself say, awestruck.

"Yes," Polly answered. "The vampire wedding color. I hope you like it."

Caitlin stepped forward, in a daze, and slowly ran her hand along its length. She had always imagined herself getting married one day, and now, for the first time, it felt real. Ever since she was little, she wondered what sort of dress she might like to be married in. She had never quite settled on any particular dress, or style—but she'd always had a feeling that it wouldn't be the typical dress.

And this certainly wasn't. This dress far surpassed anything she could have imagined. This was not a dress meant for a girl—this was a dress meant for a woman. More than a woman—a dress meant for a princess. Caitlin looked down, following the train, and saw that the fabric was studded with diamonds, and that, as they moved it, the dress glittered and sparkled in a thousand ways.

Caitlin was truly speechless. Overwhelmed with gratitude, she felt her eyes well up.

She turned and hugged Polly, then the others.

"It's beautiful," she said. "It's the most beautiful thing I have ever seen."

"Try it on!" Scarlet urged, and they all cheered.

Caitlin's tears turned into a happy laugh, as the girls helped her slip out of her robe, and held up the dress for her to step into. As she did, the girls pulled it up over her, then tied up the back with string, crisscrossing again and again. She felt increasingly tighter around her rib cage. She was shocked to realize that it fit her perfectly—as if it had been meant just for her.

Caitlin actually felt like a different person in it; she had never felt so regal in her life. She twirled and felt the material lifting into the air, swirling around her, then settling slowly back to the floor. It felt magnificent.

Caitlin could tell by the girls' stunned expressions that they were surprised by how well it fit, too.

"Amazing," Polly whispered.

"I've never seen anything like it," Taylor said. "It fits you like a glove. Incredible."

Caitlin walked over to the large mirror and stood before it, instinctively wanting to check herself.

But she saw no reflection, and remembered, too late, that it was useless. Still, she stared into the empty mirror, going through the motions she might have as a human.

"Where did it come from?" Caitlin asked.

"Aiden," Polly answered.

Caitlin turned and looked at her in surprise. She never would have expected that.

"He said he has been saving it for you for centuries. That it was always meant for you."

Caitlin was struck by that. Centuries? How long had he known that she would be getting married? Had he known from the very beginning, from the very first time she'd ever met him? She couldn't help but wonder how much he knew—and how much he knew of her future yet to come. Did he see children for her?

"Can I wear a dress like that too, Mommy?" Scarlet asked.

Caitlin smiled down at her.

"Of course you can, love. I'm sure we can have somebody make you something, right?"

The others nodded.

"How do I throw the flowers?" Scarlet persisted. "I want to practice."

The girls laughed.

"Speaking of flowers," Taylor said. "You have to choose. Which type of flowers would you like for the ceremony? And which type for the reception?"

One of the girls stepped forward and showed Caitlin several varieties of flowers: long-stem roses, all in different colors, hydrangeas, tulips….In Caitlin's eyes, they were all beautiful. She felt overwhelmed by the choice.

"Um…" Caitlin began.

"And what about the invitations?" chimed in Barbara. "Do you like this parchment, or this one?" she asked, holding up several varieties of thick, heavy parchment.

"And what sort of ink?" another girl asked. "Of course, we will seal the invitations with wax, right? Which color wax would you like?"

Caitlin's mind spun at all these details. She had never considered any of this before.

"And what color dresses would you like your bridesmaids to wear?" another girl asked.

"In the traditional vampire wedding," Polly explained, "the bride wears black, and her bridesmaids wear white. But would you like a pure white, or an off-white? Or some other color altogether?"

"And what about your groom?" asked another girl. "And his groomsmen? In most vampire weddings, they wear black velvet robes, with high collars, and a white satin shirt, with studs and cuffs. But do you want a different color scheme? And do you want him dressed differently than the others?"

"How do you want your hair?" asked another girl. "Up, or down? And what about makeup?"

"Who is Caleb's best man?" asked another.

"What sort of drinks do you want served during cocktail hour?" asked another. "We have blood-infused cocktails, and straight cocktails, and three different types of blood varieties."

"What food do you want to complement it?" asked another.

"Where you want to place the candles in the ceremony?" asked another. "And what sort of alter do you envision?"

"Have you chosen your wedding band for Caleb?" asked Polly.

Caitlin finally broke into laughter, holding up a hand.

"Enough. Please. I love you all. And I thank you so much. I don't know even where to begin. I've never considered any of this. I guess anything is fine. I don't care about the color, or the flowers, or any of these details. I just want to be married to Caleb. That's all that matters to me."

"Well, that's what we're here for," Polly said. "We'll take care of all of this for you. Is that okay?"

Caitlin nodded. "Please do. Whatever you choose, it's totally fine with me."

An excited whisper broke out among the room, as the girls started immediately debating and planning what to choose on her behalf.

"OK then," Polly said, "we'll decide on all this later. For now, let's get you out of that dress, and get our pre-wedding day rituals rolling!"

As the girls helped her get out of the dress and back into her other clothes, Caitlin looked over at Polly, puzzled.

"What rituals?" Caitlin asked.

"Why, the pre-wedding wish," Polly said, as if it were the most obvious thing in the world.

Caitlin was still puzzled.

"Before a vampire wedding," Taylor explained, "the bride is taken to a magical place, to make a wish. It's a once-in-a-lifetime event. There is a place not too far from here, where they say that whatever you wish for comes true. It's our next stop."

Caitlin knew what she would wish for—but it had already come true. To be with Caleb.

But she didn't want to disappoint his girls; if this was what was entailed in a traditional vampire wedding, she would go through with it. Besides, she wouldn't mind seeing more of the island, and getting some fresh air.

Besides, she barely had a choice. In no time at all, Caitlin found herself being dressed by all the girls in brand-new fineries, and whisked, helplessly, out the door.

*

Caleb looked out the castle window from his bedroom, watching with a smile as Caitlin was led out the castle front door, accompanied by all her bridesmaids. He could see the joy in her face, and could see how excited Scarlet was as she clung to Caitlin's side. It was a magnificent Fall day, and Caleb decided he'd go up to the roof and watch them leave, taking in the beautiful green hills, and the changing leaves. He hurried out his bedroom, down the corridor, and up a stone, twisting stairwell, leading up to the roof.

Caleb strutted across the ramparts until he reached the edge, and looked down and saw Caitlin and the others crossing the drawbridge over the moat.

"Caitlin!" he called out, cupping his hands against the wind.

Far down below, Caitlin turned and looked up, as did the girls surrounding her.

Caleb grinned wide and waved.

"I love you!" he mouthed silently.

She grinned back and waved, silently mouthing the words back. Then she was ushered away by her group of girls.

Caleb stood there, grinning, watching them all go. He couldn't be happier for her, and he was excited for their upcoming wedding. He knew this was her big girls' day, and that they'd all be busy preparing for the wedding, going through all the vampire rituals. He marveled at how few preparations the men had to go through, but figured that was the way of things.

And frankly, he was relieved not to have to worry about so many details.

Caleb was happy in this time and place. He loved being here, with Caitlin and Scarlet and Ruth and all the others, and he felt relaxed, as if he could let his guard down. The search for the final key was of course in the back of his mind, but he knew there was little that could be done until the new clue's location revealed itself to Caitlin.

Until then, they could sit back and enjoy. After all, how often did one get married? He was happy to take some time and slow down, and focus on the wedding. He just wanted things to remain the same, to go smoothly, at least until the wedding was over. After that, they could allow their mission to take them wherever it needed to go.

Caleb reflected on all the times and places he'd already been with Caitlin, and he realized, once again, how much he loved her. She had truly become a part of him; at this point, he couldn't imagine life without her. Once again, he felt a brief pang of anxiety, as he wondered what would happen once they found the final clue. Would they still be allowed to be together? What would their future look like?

As Caleb stood there, leaning against the cold stone rampart in the October morning, wondering if they would ever have a family together, suddenly, there came a voice:

"There you are."

Caleb wheeled, surprised that anyone else was up here. A part of him immediately recognized the voice, but another part refused to believe it could be possible.

Caleb's heart stopped as he turned and saw her. Sure enough, it was her. Standing there, not ten feet away, facing him. Looking as intense and passionate as she always had.

Sera.

Caleb was speechless.

She took a few, deliberate, steps forward, smiling crookedly.

"Miss me?" she asked.

Caleb started to answer, then stopped. He had no idea what to say. He was at a total loss for words. How could she possibly do this? Appear here, and now, at this time and place? When his wedding was just hours away?

Then again, he realized he shouldn't be surprised. She'd always had a way, as long as he'd known her, of appearing at the worst possible moments, of ruining anything and everything good in his life. He felt his frustration building.

"You don't have to answer," Sera continued, getting closer. "I can sense it. You miss me terribly. But you don't have to worry any longer: I'm here now."

She took a few more steps forward, and then reached up to lay a hand on his shoulder, putting on her most seductive look.

Caleb took a step back and let her hand fall in the air, not wanting to be touched by her.

"What are you doing here?" he asked coldly.

She slowly shook her head.

"That's the Caleb I always knew," she said. "Still playing hard to get. Still afraid to let your feelings for me be known. But that's okay. I know how you truly feel."

"You must leave, Sera," Caleb responded. "I'm sorry that you came, but you are not welcome here. This is our time now. Caitlin's time, and my time."

Sera scowled.

"Don't say her name in front of me," she spat. "She doesn't count. You know that. You merely turn to her because you cannot have me. I know that you long for me.

"I've arrived, before your wedding day, to save you from what you don't really want. This is your chance. Your last chance, before you make the biggest mistake of your life. Come back to me. To our home, to France. We will start a new family. We will be happy, like we'd been before."

Caleb shook his head, amazed at how deeply she still lived in fantasy, especially after all these years.

"I am truly sorry," he began, "but I have not loved you for centuries. I thought I made that clear. I'm not playing a game. I'm not playing hard to get. I sincerely do not have feelings for you anymore. So I ask respectfully that you leave me now. And that you do not return."

"Then you admit you had feelings for me once?" she asked.

Caleb thought about that. "Once. Centuries ago. Lifetimes ago."

She smiled. "That's all I needed to hear. If you had feelings for me once, you can have feelings for me again. After all, I have not changed."

"But I have," Caleb answered. "I'm not the Caleb that you once knew. I have grown, and changed. Caitlin has changed me. I love her now. I really do. And I will marry her. I look forward to marrying her. And nothing that you can say or do will ever make a difference."

"And what about our son?" Sera snapped, practically in tears. "*Jade*," she snapped again, using the name as a weapon. "Have you so conveniently forgotten about him? Does he mean nothing to you?"

Caleb felt tears well in his eyes at the thought of his son. He missed him dearly, every day, but nothing he could would bring him back now. He'd finally come to peace with that.

"I'm sorry, Sera, but Jade is gone. Nothing we can do will ever change that."

Caleb turned and began to walk away, realizing that nothing he said would change her mind, and hoping that maybe she would just disappear.

But moments later, he felt a cold hand on his shoulder, and felt it yank him, spin him back around.

Now, she was scowling, her face transformed by rage.

"You dare to disrespect me?" Sera asked. "Me? The one that you have loved for centuries?" She looked Caleb up and down, as if he were an insect. "How far you have fallen. Now you are just a pathetic creature."

"Are you finished?" Caleb asked.

Her face deepened with rage.

"No. I'm not finished. I will never be finished. No one rejects me. *No one!*" She was practically spitting the words, like a madwoman. "Today, you have made the greatest mistake of your life. If I cannot be a part of your life, then neither can she. And if you will not have me as a lover, then you will have me as an enemy. On this day, right before your wedding, I lay upon you a curse: I pronounce that I will devote the rest of my life tearing you two apart. Destroying what you have built. From here on in, I am your sworn enemy."

Caleb saw the different colors flashing in her eyes, and as he did, he felt the seriousness of her curse—and it sent a cold shiver up his spine. It was like a curse uttered from the depths of hell. And he could tell that she meant it.

Before he could open his mouth to respond, Sera suddenly turned and launched into the air, flying away, her huge black wings flapping.

As Caleb watched her rise into a fog, he felt a deepening sense of apprehension. He felt the cold and the damp rise up around him, and he knew that wherever she was flying, it couldn't possibly be good.

CHAPTER TWELVE

As Kyle swung in the air, upside down, tied by his feet to the silver rope, he looked up at Rynd—those large, lifeless black eyes, that awful scowl—and watched him swing the huge silver sword, aiming right for his throat. He knew this moment might be his last on earth. In a way, Kyle was relieved. He had been living for centuries too long, he knew that, and death might bring a peaceful reprieve.

On the other hand, as Kyle thought about it, he realized that death, in his case, would not bring a reprieve at all—but rather a quick descent into hell. He knew what he had to look forward to was a millennium of battling with demons, of being tortured by sick creatures, and he was not especially looking forward to. More importantly, he still had unfinished business on earth. He thought of Caitlin, of Caleb, of Sam, of how much he hated them all, and of how he just couldn't leave without tearing each one of them to pieces, making them suffer as he had suffered—and it gave him a whole new determination to live.

Kyle summoned one last breath, and quickly screamed out the one thing he knew that might, just might, stop Rynd from finishing his swing:

"I can lead you to the Holy Grail!"

As Kyle watched, Rynd stopped his swing in mid-air, just inches before it reached his throat. He slowly, gradually, lowered it, scowling down.

"*You*?" Rynd spat. "How?"

Kyle could see him thinking. He'd recalled that the Grail meant the world to Rynd, that he'd been obsessed with pursuing it his entire existence. Rynd had always been convinced that once he found it, he would have the secret to vampire immortality—a rare type of immortality that made even vampires impervious to any sort of attack or death—that it would make him the strongest vampire that ever lived. Kyle himself didn't believe the Grail existed—but he knew that was the bait needed to convince Rynd.

Kyle swallowed.

"Caitlin—the girl I've come back in time to find—she is on a quest for the ancient shield. And she can't find that shield without first finding the Grail. I know it to be true. Even now, her path is set in motion to find it. I've come to stop her. And I need you to help me."

"Why don't you just kill her yourself?" Rynd snarled. "Have you become that old and weak and stupid that you cannot achieve anything on your own?"

Kyle heard the vampires snicker all around him, and he felt his temper flaring. But he summoned all his reserves to keep it in check. After all, he was still, for now, at Rynd's mercy.

"She has grown powerful—stronger than you can believe. Sam, her brother, has the same skill that you do. Shapeshifting. I need someone to combat it. I need someone to use that skill against her. To dupe her, so that I can kill her once and for all."

"Well, how flattered I am," said Rynd slowly, in a mocking voice. "You mean, you felt that you could use me. For your ends."

Rynd swung the sword back slowly, preparing to strike again.

"NO!" Kyle pleaded. "Not to use you. To *help* you. You will help me get to them. And then, they will lead us to the Grail. And I will turn it over to you."

"Or maybe I'll just kill you here, and leave you to hang with the others. Food for the bats."

Kyle swallowed.

"But what good would that do you?"

Rynd leaned back and laughed, a dark, sinister laugh.

"I don't always do things for my good. Sometimes I do things just because I enjoy them."

With that, Rynd pulled back the sword, stepped forward, and brought it down in a mighty swing.

Kyle closed his eyes, feeling the air of the swing, realizing that in another split-second, he would be gone. There was nothing more he could say. This was his final moment on Earth. And to his own surprise, he was afraid.

A moment later, Kyle felt himself plunging downward, face-down, and he wondered if this was what it felt like to plunge down to hell.

But then his face hit something hard, and he realized he'd actually landed face first into the dirt.

The rest of his body followed, hitting the ground too, and as he looked up, he realized that Rynd had swung at the rope instead, cutting it. It had sent Kyle diving to the ground. Still bound, but alive.

Kyle breathed a sigh of relief.

Rynd stepped forward, his boot just missing Kyle's face, and sliced the ropes binding Kyle's feet.

Kyle immediately leapt up, to his feet, facing Rynd, red-faced and mad. But even from this perspective, standing, Rynd was huge, towering over him.

Rynd scowled down at Kyle.

"I missed you, Kyle," Rynd said. "It's been too long since I've encountered another creature as despicable as myself."

And with that, Rynd suddenly strutted right past Kyle, bumping his shoulder hard, sauntering down the dirt road, between the hundreds of hanging bodies. As he disappeared into the fog, his dozens of followers fell into line, following him.

Kyle hurried to catch up.

They walked through the fog, down a dirt road, into the twilight, and eventually the fog cleared just enough for Kyle to make out a narrow drawbridge, spanning a moat. Beyond that lay a small castle, shaped in triangle, with a single parapet, its walls low and angular. Kyle remembered the place well. Caeverlock Castle. A place for true evil. The place he knew that Rynd would be.

Kyle caught up, now walking just slightly behind Rynd, as they strutted for the castle entrance.

"You've arrived at the perfect time," Rynd said as they walked, not looking his way. "Tomorrow is the Samhain Festival. There will be plenty of slaughtering, and plenty of human captives to torture. Our favorite night of the year. "When it is finished, we will go and hunt your friends."

Rynd stopped at the castle entrance, and turned to him, his mouth widening into a smile that looked more like a scowl.

"In fact, I think I will quite enjoy it."

CHAPTER THIRTEEN

As Caitlin walked with her bridesmaids through the moss-covered hills of Skye, the sight took her breath away. The early morning sun broke low and red on the horizon, lighting up the open expanse before them. The landscape was dotted with small lakes, and the grass they walked on was a vibrant green, greener than anything she'd ever seen. It felt to her as if they had come to the very beginning of the earth, a place so pure, it hardly seemed real.

Just as Caitlin was starting to wonder where they were all hiking, Polly read her mind:

"It's called Faerie Glen," Polly said, her voice filled with excitement, even more chipper than usual. Polly practically skipped as they all headed through the countryside. "It's the only place in the world where, it is said, if you go there and make a wish, it will come true. And it's an ancient vampire ritual for a bride to make one final wish before her wedding day."

Caitlin thought about that as she rounded yet another softly sloping hill, holding Scarlet's hand, and took in another breathtaking vista. *A place to make a final wish.* But Caitlin already felt she had everything she could wish for. She had Caleb, Scarlet, Ruth, Sam, Polly, Aiden, and was surrounded by so many close friends. And now, she would be getting married. What more could she possibly want out of life?

A child. That was true. Yes, a child. With Caleb. Maybe she would wish for that.

As she walked, Caitlin felt that, finally, everything was perfect in her world. Yet, at the same time, the residue of her dream still lingered. Why did she have to have such a dream the night before such a festive day? She felt annoyed, as if Blake had somehow intruded in her dreams, had disrupted her perfect moment. She did not want to be thinking of him, or even have him lingering in a corner of her consciousness. But as she walked, several times, when she'd heard a twig snap, or a bird fly, she found herself jumping, looking to make sure that Blake wasn't standing somewhere, staring back at her. A part of her was definitely on edge. And that was not what she wanted.

She had loved Blake at one point. Had loved him dearly. But that was when she had thought Caleb was gone forever. Ever since Caleb had been back in her life, she had not thought of Blake at all. At least not consciously. *Why couldn't life be simpler?* she wondered.

As they rounded another hill, suddenly, a spectacular moss-covered valley, a lake in its center, came into view. It was the most stunning thing Caitlin had ever seen. She felt as if she'd walked straight into an oil painting, into some glowing, green fantasy land that couldn't possibly exist. She could sense the energy coming off the place. On the surface, it was just a grassy valley, beside a small, shining lake. But deep down, she sensed that it was much more— and that whatever wish she made, it would indeed come true here.

The other girls let out a gasp of excitement, and they all began to hurry down the hill, towards the lake. Polly took Caitlin's hand, and they skipped down the hill, heading for the spot to make a wish.

"You're supposed to throw a coin into the lake," Polly explained, as they raced for the shore. "If it lands heads up, your wish will come true. If not, it won't. That's the legend, anyway."

"But I don't have a coin," Caitlin said, laughing as they raced downhill.

"Don't worry," Polly said, out of breath, running beside her, "I have one for you."

"What about me?" Scarlet chimed in. "I want one, too!"

Ruth barked.

"And so does Ruth!"

Polly laughed.

They soon reached the edge of the lake and all came to a stop by its shore, out of breath, Scarlet still laughing. Caitlin looked down at the water and marveled at its light-blue, crystal-clear color: she could see right through to the bottom, and saw it was lined with thousands of smooth, multi-colored rocks. The place truly looked magical.

Polly reached into a small leather pouch and handed each of them a shining, gold coin.

"You only get one toss," Polly explained, as she placed it into their palms. "Think carefully of your wish. And make it a good one."

Caitlin looked down, opened her palm, and felt the small, cold metal in it. She then closed her eyes, and concentrated with all she had. As she did, she felt the cool October breeze caress her face, felt the slight moisture off the lake. It was dead silent here, even with all the other girls standing close by; Caitlin assumed they were all silently making a wish, too. All she could hear was the sound of the wind whipping through the ancient moss-covered hills, rippling the water. She focused, concentrating with all she had.

I wish that Caleb and I will have a child together. A child of our own.

Caitlin wished so hard, she could feel herself willing it, demanding that it come true.

She suddenly felt moisture on her cheeks. She opened her eyes, and was amazed to see that it had started to snow. She was in awe. Had the universe answered her?

She reached out and tossed the coin. She watched as it sank through the clear water and settled on the bottom. Her heart leapt to see that it landed head-first.

She felt a warm thrill run through her body, hoping beyond hope that maybe, just maybe, it could happen.

She looked over in time to see Polly toss hers and she watched as it sank down to the bottom. It landed tails-first. The hopeful expression on Polly's face collapsed into one of despair. Caitlin felt terrible for her.

"Don't worry," Caitlin said, hoping to console her, "I'm sure it's all just an old wives' tale. I'm sure whatever you wished for will come true no matter what."

But Polly looked crushed. "No it won't. It landed tails-first."

Caitlin came over and put a reassuring hand around Polly's shoulder, not knowing what to say.

"What did you wish for?" Caitlin asked.

As she looked at her, Caitlin could see that Polly was nearly in tears.

"I wished to be together with your brother, forever. That was all I wanted."

Caitlin felt a chill run through her spine at the seriousness of Polly's tone. She had never heard her sound more serious about anything since she'd known her. She could hear in her voice how much she loved Sam, how much it meant to her to be with him.

Caitlin didn't know what to say. This was the first she'd ever heard either of them express their love for each other.

As she was thinking of something to say in response, suddenly Taylor rushed over, with an alarmed expression.

"Where's Scarlet?" she asked, dread in her voice. "And Ruth?"

Caitlin's heart stopped, and she suddenly spun around wildly, searching for them. They were gone.

Caitlin couldn't understand it. Just a moment before, they had been by her side. Now, it was as if they had completely vanished. She had no idea where they could have gone in this empty landscape. Caitlin's heart started pounding.

"Scarlet!" Caitlin screamed, hearing the desperation in her own voice

Suddenly, dark clouds covered the sun, and a cold breeze ripped through the lake, blowing the snow more strongly.

And as it did, Caitlin had the sudden feeling that she would never see Scarlet again.

CHAPTER FOURTEEN

Scarlet skipped along the open meadow in high spirits, Ruth at her side. While everyone had been standing around making their wishes, she'd decided that she didn't want to make a wish after all: everything she could ever wish for, she'd realized, had already come true. She was away from that horrible, awful foster parent who had beat her in London; she was safe and sound with Caitlin and Caleb; she had new parents who she loved; and she also had Ruth, who she loved like a sister. There was nothing else Scarlet wanted in the world. So she decided she'd leave the wish-making for grown-ups.

Besides, Scarlet couldn't just stand around with everyone else, wasting time; she had important work to do. She took her role of Flower Girl seriously, and since no one was telling her exactly what to do, she figured she would decide for herself. A flower girl, she decided, had a duty to go out into the fields and find the very best flowers that the world had to offer. She had the duty to harvest them, to collect them in a basket, and to keep them safe until the day of the wedding. Scarlet didn't want her mom to have just any old flowers when she walked down the aisle: she wanted to go out and find her the very best. The most beautiful and unusual flowers anyone had ever seen. That was, she decided, her job as flower girl.

Scarlet had even brought along a special basket for this purpose, although none of the grown-ups, caught up in all their excitement, had even noticed. When they were all standing around, staring at the lake, Scarlet had seen, off in the distance, an open meadow, with some of the most beautiful, bright flowers she had ever seen. She had turned and, without thinking, had rushed off. And Ruth, of course, had followed.

Now Scarlet was in the middle of that meadow, waist high in wild flowers, picking all sorts of incredible varieties and putting them in her basket. She was already overjoyed with what she'd found. She had found red and yellow and purple and white flowers. She didn't know the names of them all, but she knew that some of them were wild roses, others were daffodils, and others were tulips. She marveled at all the different lengths and shapes and sizes, and felt proud of herself as her basket filled up.

She was skipping along, grabbing flowers left and right, when she looked up and noticed a forest in the distance. Inside the forest, she could see, were even more flowers, and some varieties which were even more colorful. They were the most beautiful things Scarlet had ever seen, and she was determined to get them for her mommy.

Scarlet hurried through the meadow and into the forest, Ruth by her side, following the trail of flowers. As she entered the canopy of trees, it suddenly grew dark; but as Scarlet wandered deeper into the woods, but she was barely aware of this. She was making incredible discoveries, and her basket was soon overflowing as she explored deeper.

Scarlet heard a noise, and stopped in her tracks. She looked all around her, at the thick and darkening wood, and suddenly felt an awareness of her surroundings that she didn't have before. She realized that maybe she had made a mistake coming this deep into the woods, so far from her Mommy and the others. She turned about in all directions, and suddenly felt a bit unsure about precisely which way she had come from. And she couldn't see the way out, either. All she saw, everywhere, were trees.

The noise came again, and Scarlet stiffened, scared. Several branches snapped, and Scarlet spotted motion in a clump of bushes about twenty feet away.

The noise was followed by a deep, guttural snarl.

Scarlet want to turn and run, but she was frozen in fear, too afraid to move, and not knowing which way to run. The snarl grew deeper, and suddenly, she saw several huge shapes appear from behind a bush. Her heart nearly stopped.

It was a pack of wolves.

These wolves looked nothing like Ruth. They were huge, enormous, twice her size, nearly the size of bears. They also looked skinny, famished, and their lips were curled back in vicious scowls. Their eyes gleamed yellow, and they held in them nothing but death. There were a half dozen of them, and their eyes all locked on Scarlet.

Scarlet felt paralyzed in their sites, and had no idea what to do. She realized instantly that she could never outrun them, and that she had made a big mistake in coming here alone.

Beside her, Ruth snarled back. It was a loud, vicious warning noise, a scarier noise than Scarlet had ever heard Ruth make before. Ruth took several steps forward, standing in front of Scarlet, protecting her, snarling back at the pack. Scarlet was grateful for her protection. But not reassured. Ruth was badly outnumbered, and these wolves, so enormous, were each twice her size.

Yet still, Ruth was fearless. After a series of the most vicious warning snarls Scarlet had ever heard, it was clear the wolves were not backing off—and that was when Ruth burst into action.

She chose the biggest wolf, one that seemed to be the leader, and charged right for him.

With just a few strides, Ruth leapt into the air, and managed to sink her teeth squarely into the wolf's throat. The other wolf seemed surprised, as if he hadn't expected Ruth to be so bold and daring. Ruth's teeth lodged deep into his throat, as the two wrestled on the ground.

Another wolf came running over and attacked Ruth from the side, sinking its fangs into her back. But Ruth would not let go of her deadly grip. The leader rolled on his back, clawing at Ruth, trying to get her off. But it was no use. Ruth had death in her eyes, and she clamped down with such power, that within moments, the leader was dead.

But Ruth paid the price. Two more wolves jumped on her, and all three wolves managed to bring her down to the ground. They were all on top of her, clawing and biting; Ruth, on her back, fought back valiantly. But a fourth jumped on her, and she was just too badly outnumbered.

Scarlet felt a sense of desperation. The other wolf had her in his sights, and he suddenly burst into a sprint, right for her.

Scarlet turned and ran, knowing, even as she did, that it was useless. She barely got a few feet when she felt the first clawing on her back. It was long, and razor-sharp, and it struck her with such speed, that she felt it slicing open her skin. It tore right through her clothing, and across her shoulder blade, and the force of it sent her flying, face first, to the ground.

Scarlet didn't even have a chance to turn around. A split second later, the wolf was on top of her, its awful snarls in her ears, filling her entire universe, its hot breath in her face, its filthy claws on her back. Her world was spinning, and in a moment of clarity, she knew that suddenly, just like that, her life was about to be over.

Out of the corner of her eye, she watched helplessly as the wolf opened its mouth and lowered its large, yellow fangs right for her throat. Then she felt awful pain as the three inch-long fangs broke her skin and sunk into her neck. She felt more pain than she knew was possible, then felt her own blood rushing out of her, as her world began to spin, growing lighter and lighter.

The last thing she saw, before her world went black, was her basket of flowers, sprawled out on the forest floor. And her final thought, before her life ended, was that she wished she could gather them back up again, and just have one chance to show them to her Mommy.

CHAPTER FIFTEEN

Caitlin sprinted through the open meadow, beside herself with grief and anxiety. How could she have been so stupid to take her eyes off of Scarlet? She blamed herself for not being a better parent. She should have had more of an instinct to keep an eye on Scarlet every second. And now Scarlet was missing, and she felt it was entirely her fault.

She ran through the meadow, Polly and the girls at her side, all calling Scarlet's name, all scanning the grass, all equally frantic. Caitlin couldn't help but wonder if they all blamed her, too. After all, Scarlet was now her daughter— whether by blood or not. She was her responsibility. It was selfish of her to have closed her eyes for that long, to take time to make her wish.

But then again, she reasoned, she couldn't have expected it. She had never known Scarlet to be the type to just run off like that, unannounced, without any warning. Caitlin still couldn't understand why she did. If there was any consolation, it was that Ruth was nowhere to be found either, and thus must be with

Scarlet. Caitlin felt slightly consoled by that. Ruth would never allow anything bad to happen to her.

"No one blames you," Polly said, as she hurried quickly by her side, scanning the field. She must have read her thoughts. "You didn't do anything wrong."

Caitlin was too upset to even respond, but deep down, she felt she had. She also felt completely unnerved that Scarlet should have disappeared at the exact moment that she had been wishing to have a family of her own. She had been warned that Faerie Glen was a powerful place, a place where all wishes came true, and she had sensed that herself. Had her wish, she wondered, somehow set something in motion? Did her wishing to have a family with Caleb somehow put into motion Scarlet's being taken away from her? Had she somehow endangered Scarlet?

Caitlin felt torn, wracked with emotions. Why did this have to happen now, she wondered, the day before her wedding? She wished she had never gone to that lake, never made that wish. She wished desperately that she could start over, do everything differently. She had been so wrapped up in herself, and her stupid wedding preparations, that she had just not been vigilant enough. She would never forgive herself.

"SCARLET!" Caitlin shrieked again, for the millionth time, as she scanned the horizon, the fields, the sky. The snow poured down, thicker by the moment, and started to accumulate beneath her feet.

High up in the sky, a vulture screeched back, as if mocking her. Caitlin looked up and noticed the dark, thick clouds gathering on the horizon, and she couldn't help feeling as if the whole world were in mourning.

Caitlin scanned the horizon once again, willing the universe to show her where Scarlet could be. She had no idea where she could have disappeared to so quickly. All the other girls were bent over, scanning the grass, as if Scarlet might have collapsed, might be hidden in the tall grass. The thought made Caitlin's heart hurt.

Suddenly, there was a shuffling of feet behind her, and Caitlin turned, hopefully, expectantly, praying that it was Scarlet, running to her arms.

But it was not. It was Caleb, running towards them. Taylor had gone back to find him, to tell him the news, and they had returned. Now here he was, a frown on his face, looking more concerned than Caitlin had ever seen him. He looked as if he had aged overnight.

Caitlin hoped that he didn't blame her.

"Where is she?" Caleb asked urgently.

Caitlin shook her head, wiping a tear from her eye.

He hugged Caitlin. It felt momentarily good to be in his arms, reassuring, as if his rippling muscles could stop any trouble in the world. But as Caitlin pulled away, she knew that this time, that would not be the case.

Caleb scanned the horizon desperately, his face etched with concern. Caitlin was about to continue walking through the meadow, but she changed her mind. Instead, she stopped. She felt it was time for a different approach. It was time to draw on her innate power, her senses, on everything Aiden had ever taught her.

She closed her eyes and tuned in, turning her palms up, feeling the air, feeling the moisture in it, feeling the soil beneath her feet. She breathed deep and tried to become one with the universe, with everything around her. She felt a soft breeze tickling her face, felt the flakes of snow on her cheek, listened deeply to the slightest sound the insects were making. She willed for herself to become one with the universe, willed for the universe to reveal to her were Scarlet might possibly be.

Caitlin stood there for she didn't know how long, losing all sense of time and space.

And then suddenly, she had an insight.

She opened her eyes and scanned the horizon. There. In the distance. That clump of trees.

"There!" Caitlin suddenly yelled, pointing.

The others stopped, rose to their feet, and looked to where she was pointing.

"She's in those woods," Caitlin screamed again, then took off at a sprint.

Caleb and the others were right behind her, sprinting as fast as she.

*

As Caitlin burst into the woods, the sky darkening under the canopy of the foliage, she immediately sensed that something was wrong. She sensed it as a mother. It felt as if one of her own limbs had been severed. A chill ran up her spine as she burst deeper into the forest, filled with a sense of foreboding.

As she ran, she noticed a trail of torn flowers spread out, and as she looked more carefully, she saw they were spotted in blood. She felt a pit in her stomach, as her sense of foreboding deepened.

She did not even need to turn the corner to know what lay just around it. Every pore in her body screamed to her that something was terribly, irrevocably, wrong.

As she turned the corner, and saw the sight, she collapsed to her knees, and let out a wail of grief unlike any she had before.

There, on the forest trail, sprawled out before, covered in blood, was Scarlet. Her daughter.

And just feet away from her, covered in blood, lying on her side, whimpering and barely moving, was Ruth.

Caitlin saw blood everywhere, but it was all blurry, out of focus. Her world was spinning as she sank to her knees in the snow, in the soft forest floor, wailing over Scarlet's little body. Caitlin was afraid to, but she turned Scarlet over anyway.

Caitlin's grief deepened, if that were possible. Scarlet's lifeless face stared back, her eyes opened, unblinking. Caitlin felt for a pulse, but there was none. She was dead.

Caitlin saw the deep bite marks in her throat, saw the blood all over her, and knew that she had met a horrific death, that there was no possible way anyone could have survived whatever attacked her. Caitlin leaned back and shrieked, her wail of grief rising up into the sky, just as Caleb, Polly, Taylor, and all the others hurried over and stood over her, staring down, gaping.

"Scarlet!" Caitlin cried, feeling she had nothing left to live for.

She reached down and picked her up, cradling in her arms, hugging her tight to her chest. Caitlin could feel her little body in her arms, and at that moment, she would give anything, *anything*, to bring her back.

"I would do anything!" Caitlin yelled up to the sky. "Do you hear me!?" she screamed out to the universe, like a mad woman. "Anything. I would give up anything to have Scarlet back again. I VOW! ANYTHING!"

Suddenly, a gale force wind ripped through the trees. The snow whipped around her, and the clouds shifted, letting in a ray of sunlight through the deep and dark wood. In the distance, on the forest trail, there appeared a lone figure, walking towards them.

Caitlin looked up, barely able to see with the tears in her eyes.

Aiden.

He walked slowly and gravely towards her, cloaked in his long robe and hood, leaning on his ancient staff as he went. In moments, he was standing over her.

Caitlin looked up with tearful eyes, hoping beyond hope that maybe, just maybe, there was something he could do.

But from his grave look, she didn't take much hope.

"You must help us," Caitlin pleaded. "Please. You *must*. You have to bring her back. You *have* to!"

Suddenly, Caitlin felt a squirming in her arms. She looked down and her heart stopped as she saw Scarlet, eyes now closed, flinch just the slightest bit. She held her breath, watching, hoping it would happen again.

It did. Scarlet was twisting and moving her arms. Caitlin's heart soared, afraid to hope.

Could it be?

A moment later, as all the others crowded around, Scarlet suddenly opened her eyes. She stared right back at Caitlin.

"Mommy," she said, her voice soft, "my neck hurts."

Caitlin hugged Scarlet tightly, rocking her back and forth, tears running down her face, overjoyed to see her alive, moving, breathing, talking. It felt like a dream.

Caitlin was so confused. She didn't understand how it could be possible. Just a moment ago, Scarlet was clearly dead. She was sure of it.

But as Scarlet's little hands hugged her back, Caitlin didn't care. She didn't need to know how it happened. All she cared about was that she was back with her again.

"I'm so sorry," Caitlin said, over and over, crying. "I'm so sorry. I'll never leave you again."

Caitlin gradually looked up, and saw Aiden still standing over them, staring down. She felt a debt of gratitude, and wonder.

"How did you do it?" Caitlin asked. "How did you bring her back?"

Aiden slowly shook his head, as the entire crowd looked to him.

"You still don't understand," he said softly. "I didn't bring her back. She never died. Only mortals die," he added, and then as he turned his back, he said his final words, words that Caitlin would never forget, "and Scarlet is no mortal. She is a vampire. And she is your daughter."

CHAPTER SIXTEEN

Kyle hiked with Rynd and his men up a rocky hill on the Isle of Lewis. It had been a long flight to get here, and as they had flown over the Isle of Skye, Kyle had wondered about the wisdom of Rynd's plan. Kyle had wanted to just dive down right there and launch a direct attack on Skye. But Rynd had insisted that was not the best approach; he had claimed that Skye was protected from vampire attack by an invisible shield. Rynd had suggested another, more devious, way.

They had been hiking for hours, and Rynd had offered few details of his plan. Kyle was not used to following, to taking orders, and he was reaching his limit. Indeed, just as he was getting ready to confront Rynd again, finally Rynd hiked up alongside him.

"Tonight is the Samhain Festival," Rynd said. "Our kind will flock here from around the world. It is our night for power, the one night when evil has free reign. We will use the energy of this night to summon our evil cohorts from every corner of the earth. Whatever creatures are out there, they will come to us, like moths to a flame. Then, tomorrow, we will attack Skye as one."

Kyle looked at him, puzzled.

"But I thought you said Skye had a shield, was immune to attack—"

"We can't lead a head-on attack. But I can use my shapeshifting powers to trick one of them into inviting us. With a formal invitation, the gates will be opened. Then our entire army can attack."

Kyle looked at Rynd with a new admiration. Of course. The sacred vampire invitation. One vampire coven could not cross water to attack another coven. Unless they were invited. And with Rynd's shapeshifting power, he could deceive someone, and get an invitation.

Kyle smiled broadly. He knew there was a reason he'd wanted to use his old apprentice. He had known, he had just *known*, that Rynd would be the key.

And Kyle liked his plan. Of course. Samhain. There was no better day of the year to harness the evil forces of the universe. Kyle recalled his heyday, when they would spend entire days leading up to, during, and after Samhain, sacrificing humans, drinking their blood, and on all-night orgies of sex and witchcraft and bloodshed. It was his favorite day of the year. With all of Rynd's men in attendance, they could collectively perform ceremonies and rituals and sacrifices that could help conjure up even the most evil of spirits. Yes, Kyle was feeling optimistic. It was a very propitious sign indeed.

But Kyle was still uncertain of why Rynd had chosen the Isle of Lewis to celebrate Samhain.

And then they rounded a hill, and Kyle saw it: the Callanish Stones. Of course. Kyle hadn't thought of these for centuries. But now that he saw them, it made perfect sense. There was no better place Rynd could have picked.

The Callanish Stones had been around for thousands of years, and were an ancient power spot for vampires. Laid out in a crude circle, they looked like the stones of Stonehenge, except these stones were more narrow, haphazard. They sat atop a dramatic knoll, on a remote island, overlooking cliffs and a vast ocean. They were eerie, and exuded a mystical power.

As they approached, a sudden gale force wind met them, and Kyle could already sense the power of this place. There was nothing more he could have asked for: the Samhain Festival. The Callanish Stones. Rynd and his coven....It was a sure recipe for victory. This time, Caitlin would be his.

As Kyle walked with the others to the circle of stones, he could hear shrieks in the distance. He looked over and saw several of Rynd's men, sadistic smiles on their faces, dragging a human—a woman—with long blonde hair. They tore off her clothes, until she was naked, and dragged her to the center of the circle, propping her against a rock. As they held her in place, Rynd walked up, extracted a knife, and in one motion, reached down and sliced her throat.

Blood gushed everywhere, and dozens of Rynd's men rushed in, kneeling and feeding. Rynd lifted the blade, and licked it clean.

Kyle felt his heart warm. He knew that this was going to be the start of a wonderful night.

CHAPTER SEVENTEEN

Caitlin, still holding a sleeping Scarlet in her arms, walked with Caleb through the forest trail, following Aiden. Caleb held Ruth, who was severely injured, but still alive. It seemed that she might make it—albeit with a large scar across her face from where she'd been attacked.

They followed Aiden silently through the twisting and turning forest trail, deep into the woods. The others had gone back to the castle, at Aiden's request, leaving them alone. There was something Aiden needed to discuss with them, and clearly he wanted privacy.

As they walked, Caitlin was just so grateful to have Scarlet back, alive. Her mind was still reeling with the news. Scarlet. A vampire. Her daughter. There were so many questions she was burning to ask Aiden. But for now she just wanted to revel in the fact that Scarlet was still alive.

And that she was her daughter.

Caitlin had never been more overjoyed. Deep down, she had always sensed this to be true—Scarlet, her daughter. Their bond had been so deep, so immediate, and she had thought so many times that she saw herself in the child. Yet she was shocked to actually hear it. It seemed that Caleb was shocked, too: he kept looking over at Scarlet with such deep affection, stroking her hair, and he seemed overwhelmed by the fact that he had a daughter. A *real* daughter.

Caitlin couldn't help but think that her wish, at Faerie Glen, had really come true.

The woods opened up, the sun dramatically broke through the clouds, and stretched out before them was the edge of a cliff. On the horizon, there was an expanse of ocean.

Aiden went over and leaned against one of these, his back to them, looking out at the sky.

Aiden sighed, holding his staff, looking ancient as he gazed out at the expanse of ocean. Several minutes of silence passed, and Caitlin wondered if he was ever going to speak. Finally, he began.

"Scarlet is your daughter, the result of your union. You had her in the future. She traveled back in the past to be with you. She has no memory of this, and never will. But she is the daughter you never lived to see in the future.

"Back in Pollepel, you made a decision to give up everything to go back in time, to do whatever you could to save Caleb's life. Even your unborn child. Now, that decision has been rewarded. Here and now, you are finally getting back what you had lost.

"Scarlet is no ordinary child. She is unlike any other vampire. She is far more evolved, and can sense and see things more deeply. As she grows, so will her powers. Beyond what you could ever imagine. You must watch her closely. At all times. Protect her with all that you have."

"I will," Caitlin responded, and meant it. She sensed she was being rebuked for taking her eyes off of her earlier.

"When you found Scarlet in the woods, you made a vow. Vampire vows are sacred. Any and every vow must be exacted. You vowed you would do anything, give up anything, to have her back. Yes, she is immortal. But at the same time she had a destiny. Your love is what brought her back. It changed her destiny. And yours."

Aiden turned and looked at her.

"You vowed that you would give up anything. And that vow will be exacted. You will, indeed, have to give up something. Something dearly precious to you."

Caitlin felt her heart pounding. "What?" she asked, afraid to know the answer.

But Aiden just turned and looked away, back to the ocean.

"I'm afraid that will be for you to discover. The wheels of fate."

Caitlin was horrified. What had she done?

"It's not Caleb, is it? I won't have to give him up, will I?"

Aiden shook his head.

"No. But it will be something equally precious to you."

Caitlin wracked her brain, with another pang of dread. Still, she would give up anything to have Scarlet back, and she was prepared to pay any price.

"Tomorrow is your wedding day," Aiden pronounced. "A very sacred time in the vampire universe. It was destined for you to know this about Scarlet before you two exchanged your vows. When the wedding is over, the next morning, you must resume your mission. Find the fourth key as soon as possible. Something dangerous is happening in the vampire world. There is an urgency. Do not delay."

Caitlin watched as Aiden closed his eyes with a look of concern; clearly he was sensing something terrible on the way, watching some awful future unfold.

"What's going to happen?" Caitlin asked in a whisper, almost wishing he wouldn't reply.

Aiden merely shook his head.

Caitlin turned and looked at Caleb, and they exchanged a look of mutual concern. Then she looked back at Aiden. And to her complete shock, he was gone.

Vanished.

Caitlin and Caleb looked at each other, dumbfounded.

Caitlin's mind was spinning. She felt overwhelmed by the implications of it all. Scarlet, their daughter. Back from another time. Her vow. The threat of her losing something precious. Tomorrow, her wedding day. Resuming the mission. The trouble brewing in the vampire universe. Her mind spun.

And then, to make matters worse, Caleb suddenly looked at her gravely, and she could see in his eyes that he had something he was afraid to tell her. Her heart started pounding. She didn't know how much more she could take.

"I received a visitor," Caleb said, clearing his throat, "right before I came to you. Sera. She came back in time looking for me."

Caitlin's heart was thumping in her chest, as her mouth went dry.

No, she thought. *Not now. Not with only a day to go.*

Caleb shook his head. "I sent her away. I promise you. You have to trust me. I thought you should know. I also thought you should know that she cursed us, vowed to tear us apart. I do not fear her. But I do fear for Scarlet. We must watch her very carefully."

Caitlin had to walk. It was all too much for her, and she felt her blood running cold. Now this. Caleb and Sera. Why had she visited him? Did he still have feelings for her?

Caitlin couldn't help but think of her dream the night before, of Blake. Of his lingering in her consciousness. Did Sera linger in Caleb's consciousness, too?

Caitlin desperately needed time alone, to process all of this. She didn't want to say anything, for fear that she would regret it. So she clutched Scarlet, still sleeping in her arms, and suddenly turned.

"I need some time alone," she said.

With that, she took three big steps and leapt into the air, flying over the island, into the horizon, and far, far away from Caleb.

CHAPTER EIGHTEEN

Caitlin walked along the sandy shore, holding Scarlet's hand, the ocean waves crashing just feet away. It was a desolate and bleak shoreline, stretching as far as the eye could see, the dark gray sea blending into a horizon of gray clouds. The colors matched Caitlin's mood. As always in her life, just when everything seemed to be so going so great, things took a sudden and dramatic turn for the worse.

She supposed that she should be grateful. After all, Scarlet was alive. That, really, was all that mattered. And she was more grateful for that than she could ever express. In fact, Caitlin squeezed her hand more tightly as they walked, afraid to ever let it go.

Just as she was reeling from the trauma of the event, from Aiden's pronouncement of a terrible loss yet to come, she also had to hear this news about Sera. Caleb's timing was terrible, though at the same time, she did appreciate his not keeping it from her. At least she had managed to wisely hold her tongue this time, and give herself time to cool down. She was proud of herself for not saying something she would regret, or taking hasty action, or rushing to blame Caleb for the situation.

Now that she was away from him, breathing the salty ocean air, walking with Scarlet, her head was beginning to clear. She was starting to realize that it was not Caleb's fault, and there was nothing to blame him for. Yes, it was beyond annoying that Sera persisted in interfering in their lives. Yes, it bothered her that Sera had vowed to tear them apart. Of course, that was news that no bride would wish for on the day before her wedding.

But at the same time, Caleb was hers now. At least, that was how Caitlin felt. She wore his ring, and whether they'd had the ceremony yet or not, she felt that deep down, their souls were connected. After all, she was holding Scarlet's hand, their child's hand. What more proof could she want than that?

As she walked, her bare feet sinking into the sand, she realized she should let go of any upset with Caleb. Sera was really the one to blame. If anything, she should be grateful to Caleb for always deflecting Sera's advances, and for being so honest with her.

Most importantly, Caitlin realized there was nothing to fear: there was no way Sera could ever tear them apart. Caleb loved her, Caitlin. She felt it. And nothing—and no one—could ever take that away. The more she dwelled on it, the more her anger toward Sera started to abate. She realized that Sera was just a powerless, pathetic creature, a lost woman who was unable to get on with her own life.

Caitlin's thoughts turned to Scarlet. She looked down at her, and marveled at how peaceful and content she seemed, skipping in the sand, looking out at the sea, chasing the seabirds running along the shore. She felt so connected to her. Caitlin was overwhelmed to think that Scarlet was hers. Her daughter. Her *real* daughter. And now that she knew she was her mother, she felt a greater responsibility than ever. To guide her, to teach her who she was, what it meant to not be of the human race. Caitlin recalled when she had first found out she, herself, wasn't human; it had been quite a shock.

"Mommy?" Scarlet suddenly asked, kicking a seashell, "what is a vampire?"

Caitlin felt a chill. Scarlet's timing was uncanny. She could not believe how easily she'd read her thoughts.

"Well," Caitlin began, trying to think of how to explain this to a child, of how to choose her words, "a vampire is a very special person. One that has special talents and abilities. One that has a special way of eating, and one that can live a very, very long time."

Scarlet furrowed her brow. "Longer than other types of people?"

"Oh yes," Caitlin said. "A lot longer."

"Is that what I am?" she asked. "A vampire?"

Caitlin looked down at her shining eyes, looking up at her, and knew that she had to be completely honest. Children demanded that.

"Yes, honey, you are. And, in your case, that is a very beautiful thing."

"Are you one, too? Is Daddy?"

"Yes," she said. "We all are. Our whole family."

"Does that mean that we all get to live a long time? Together?"

Caitlin stopped and knelt down, and looked her in the eyes.

"I sure hope so," she said.

Scarlet frowned.

"But I heard that vampires are scary. Does that mean I'm scary?"

Caitlin smiled.

"No, love, you're not scary at all. You're perfect. Only some vampires are scary. Just like some humans are scary. Other vampires are very, very nice. Even nicer than some humans."

"Is that my kind?" Scarlet asked.

"Yes it is. We never hurt any humans. We eat animals, just like humans eat animals."

Scarlet seemed to relax a little bit.

"When those wolves attacked me," Scarlet began, "I felt them biting me. I felt their teeth in my neck. And then everything went black. I was sure that I was dead. It was like I was supposed to be dead. But I didn't die. I don't understand. Does that mean that I can't ever die?"

Scarlet stared back at her intensely, and Caitlin could see that she desperately wanted the truth.

Caitlin cleared her throat, and looked her in the eyes.

"You are like your Mommy and Daddy. Which means that you can't die. Not like humans die."

Scarlet looked down at the sand, then off at the water, as if debating how to react. Finally, she looked back at Caitlin.

"I always knew I was different. Sometimes, I can hear things. Not like normal people. It's like… I can hear people's thoughts. Like yours, sometimes. When I try to." She looked at Caitlin. "Is that strange?"

Caitlin knelt down and smiled at her, brushing the hair out of her face.

"You're not strange. You just have very special gifts. And you may have even more gifts, ones that we don't even know about yet. But that doesn't mean you're strange. It just means that you're special. Like us."

"Like *all* of us," came a voice.

Caitlin wheeled, shocked at the sound of the strange, male voice so close behind her, and immediately protective of Scarlet. Caitlin didn't understand how anyone could have crept up on her, especially here, in the middle of nowhere.

Until, that is, she saw the face staring back at her. And her jaw nearly dropped open.

Standing there, a foot away from her, was Blake.

*

Caitlin stared, speechless. Blake looked exactly as he did the last time she saw him: he still had those perfect, chiseled features, the longish, wavy brown hair, the large, green eyes and that far-off, distant look, like a haunted loner.

Blake. It was really him. She thought of her dream the night before. Had it been more than just a coincidence? Had he visited her in her dreams? Of all people, alone on this desolate beach, why did it have to be him? And why now, just as she was sorting through her feelings for Caleb, just as she was preparing for her wedding day?

He stared back at her, and a slight smile formed at the corner of his lips.

"Hello, Caitlin," he said in his soft voice.

Scarlet stood between them, and Caitlin could sense her curiosity, as she looked back and forth between them, trying to figure it all out.

"Hello, Blake," she answered flatly.

Caitlin didn't know what to say. She felt herself trembling inside, torn by a million conflicting emotions. She wanted to thank him for saving her life; to apologize to him for all that she'd put him through; she even felt the need to apologize to him for marrying Caleb.

But most of all, she just wanted him to stop looking at her that way, with those intense eyes that prevented her from looking anywhere else, from thinking of anything else. She thought back to their first time together, on Pollepel, of their standing guard together on that sunken parapet in the river. On the one hand, it felt like lifetimes ago; on the other, it felt like it was just yesterday.

She had to forcibly shake herself out of it, to remind herself that she was with Caleb now. That Blake was lifetimes ago. That was the problem with vampire relationships and with immortality: nothing seemed to ever stay in the past. People and relationships always came back, full circle, again and again, no matter when and where you were. Nothing ever died. Ever.

"Your wedding is tomorrow," he stated flatly.

She wasn't quite sure how to respond. She felt nervous and guilty the same time.

"I'm happy for you," he added.

"Thank you," she said, trying to stay calm.

"Who's that, Mommy?" Scarlet asked, tugging on her pants, pointing at Blake.

Caitlin wasn't sure how to respond.

Before she could, Blake looked down and smiled at her. He walked over to the shoreline, collected a handful of small rocks, and gestured to Scarlet. She came over to him.

He reached over and handed her a few of them, as she opened her palm.

"Do you see these?" he asked.

She nodded back, studying the rocks.

"Choose the ones that are flat. Like this one," he said, taking one of his and placing it in her palm.

"Then throw them like this, sideways."

Blake reached out and threw the rock into the waves, and it skipped along the water. It jumped several times, and as it did, Scarlet squealed in delight.

Scarlet tried to copy him, but it didn't work. He corrected her grip.

"You need to just skim the surface of the water. Don't throw it straight down. Try to throw it sideways."

Scarlet tried a second and third time, and it still didn't work. But the fourth time, she managed to get it to skip once. She screamed in delight.

"Mommy mommy! Look what I did! The rock bounced off the water!"

Caitlin couldn't help but smile as Scarlet burst into action, picking up as many rocks as she could find, and trying again and again.

Blake stood, watching her, smiling. Then slowly, he came back to Caitlin.

"Do you miss me?" he asked, softly. She could see the sadness and intensity in his eyes, and she could feel how much he missed her.

She checked her feelings, and realized that somewhere, deep in her consciousness, she did miss him. She did, from time to time, think of their days together, no matter how much she tried to push them away.

At the same time, she loved Caleb. Not partially, as with Blake. But entirely. She may have thought of Blake from time to time, but she didn't actively pine for him. She didn't feel as if she needed him, or anyone else, to be complete, to give her anything that was missing. She felt entirely complete with Caleb. The residue of Blake might still linger somewhere in her past, but, she realized, that was natural. The way she figured, anyone in life who at one time means anything to you is bound to leave some sort of impression. But that didn't mean that she was still devoted to him. Nor did it mean that she was betraying Caleb. She was finally beginning to realize that the two could co-exist in her consciousness; if she tried to drive occasional thoughts of Blake out, and they just wouldn't go away, it didn't mean that she was doing anything wrong. Or that she was still attached to him.

She did realize, though, that even if she didn't have control over her deepest, unconscious thoughts and impressions, she did, very much, have power and control over her conscious thoughts, choices, actions, and her words. She had a responsibility to discipline herself to not actively think of Blake, to let any passing thoughts of him go without dwelling on them, and to instead choose to actively focus on Caleb. She also had a responsibility to choose her words carefully, and to communicate clearly to Blake, so that there would be no confusion on his part.

"What we had, at the time, was beautiful," Caitlin said. "And I don't want to upset you. But you need to realize, for both of our sakes, that it's over. It's gone forever, and will never come back. If we go searching for it, it won't be there. We need to let it go. You need to let it go. I love Caleb now. I'm devoted to him. And nothing will ever change that."

Blake looked at her for a long time, and she could tell he was really hearing her, really taking it in. Finally, slowly, he nodded, then turned and looked out at the ocean.

"Mommy, look!" Scarlet screamed. "I got it to skip four times!"

Caitlin saw Blake's sad smile as he watched Scarlet. She turned and looked over at Scarlet herself.

Scarlet held up a rock for her to try. Caitlin walked over, grabbed the rock, and threw it, thinking back to her own childhood, of skipping rocks with Sam at a lake somewhere upstate.

The rock skipped several times, and Scarlet screamed in delight. Caitlin turned, proud of herself, eager to see Blake's expression. But to her surprise, he was already gone.

Vanished.

Caitlin spun and looked up at the sky. The sunset had finally broken through, lighting the world in a million soft colors. In the distance, she could just barely spot a lone figure, flapping his huge wings, and flying alone, desperately, into the horizon of light, and as she watched him go, something told her that was the last time she would ever see Blake again.

CHAPTER NINETEEN

Sam stood on a remote corner of the Isle of Skye, Polly beside him, atop a grassy knoll, overlooking an endless expanse of sea. Beneath them, waves crashed against huge primordial boulders, and above them, the sky was lit up by one of the most beautiful sunsets he had ever seen. The sky was so big here, he felt dwarfed by the enormity of it.

He had been walking with Polly for hours, and they had finally settled on this spot. She had come to him earlier in the day, shaken, and had told him everything that had happened with Scarlet and the wolves. Sam had been shocked by the story, and he could understand how disturbing it must have been for Polly. The thought of almost losing Scarlet had disturbed her, as did the revelation that Scarlet was Caitlin and Caleb's daughter. It took Polly hours of talking about it to finally calm down. Sam sensed that she needed to talk, to vent all her feelings, and he let her talk.

"The wedding is tomorrow, and I feel like there's so much left for me to do," Polly said.

"I'm the maid of honor, after all. Caitlin took off, and she honestly doesn't seem that concerned with all the details. It seems like she'll be happy no matter what, and I know the other girls have already taken care of all the last-second arrangements, so I guess I shouldn't worry. But still. I know I should be there....but I wanted to spend time with you."

They sat on the grass, facing each other against the sky, and Sam felt his heart warm at her words. She had wanted to see him. *Him.* Of all people. He was the first one she came to. It made him feel special. Needed.

Polly, talking herself out about the day's events, now seemed to focus on him.

"Thanks for listening," she said. "Sorry I talked so long."

"It's okay," Sam said. "I can listen to you talk for hours."

Polly leaned in and they kissed.

Sam felt his desire for her coursing through his veins, and he could sense the same in her.

"Did you mean all those things you said yesterday?" Polly asked, tentatively. "About how much you love me?"

"I did," Sam said. "And I do."

They kissed again, longer, more passionately.

"The first time I saw you," Polly began, breaking into a shy smile, "I liked you from the start. There was something endearing about you.

But I guess I kind of put it out of my head, because you were my best friend's brother. I thought...I don't know...I thought that might be a problem." She looked into Sam's eyes, "But to be honest, I never stopped thinking about you."

Sam felt his heart soar at her words. It felt so good to hear her say the very thing that was on his mind.

"I never stopped thinking about you, either," Sam replied.

Sam was about to lean in for a kiss, but suddenly, her brow furrowed.

"What's wrong?" he asked.

She looked away, and as she did, he could see how upset she was.

"I made a wish today," she said. "At Faerie Glen." Then she fell into a gloomy silence.

"And?" Sam prodded. "What did you wish for?"

She shot him a look. "You're not supposed to ask that," she said.

Sam felt embarrassed. "Sorry," he said.

Polly sighed. "My point is...the coin...it landed tails down." She looked at him. "My wish can't come true."

"That's just superstition," Sam dismissed.

Polly shook her head, and he could tell she was really troubled by it. Finally, she turned to him.

"Do you think that, if we're destined to be together, then we will be? I mean, like, forever?"

Forever. The word reverberated in Sam's mind, like a bell going off.

But it didn't scare him. It surprised him to hear her say it, because it was such an intense thing to say, especially so early in the relationship. And it surprised him even more, because that was the exact thought that had been going through his own mind.

Forever.

That was what he wanted, too.

Sam couldn't tell if he was feeling this way just because it was so fresh, his being in love with Polly—or if it was because it was true love.

Deep down, he felt that it was true love. That it was what he truly wanted.

"I do," Sam said. "And there's nothing I'd like more."

Polly's face broke into an enormous smile, outshining the final rays of the sun. She leaned in and kissed him, and moments later the two of them were rolling in the soft grass, kissing each other, their desire reaching a fever pitch. As they rolled in the grass, and twilight began to fall, Sam knew that the time had arrived for them to finally become one.

CHAPTER TWENTY

As Kyle stood with Rynd's man amidst the circle of Callanish Stones, watching the blood red sun set, he had never been so content. Here he was, back in ancient Scotland, standing in a place of pure vampire power, on the Samhain Festival, the darkest day of the year, and surrounded by scores of fellow vampires just as sadistic as he. Finally, he felt at home.

He looked around, and saw Rynd's men torturing and slaughtering one innocent human after another, feasting on their blood, tearing them from limb to limb. Kyle had feasted himself, all afternoon, as the sun had slowly set, and he felt more gorged than he had in centuries. It was already the start of an amazing night.

And the best was yet to come. As the blood red sun filled the entire sky, Kyle turned and faced it, held out his arms, and slowly felt the power of Samhain infusing his body, rising up from his toes. This was truly the power night of his kind. For thousands of years on this day, humans had celebrated witchcraft, tried to raise the dead, had tortured and slaughtered other humans. Eventually, the humans would water it down, call it "Halloween," and turn it into a night of mere mischief.

But now, back in the 12th century, this day was still what it was meant to be: a time of true, demonic evil. Kyle knew that demons were granted permission to walk the earth on this night, and he felt them swirling all around him, lending him power, urging him to kill, to torture. He opened his arms wide, leaned his head back to the sky, and felt their power coursing through him.

All around him torches were being lit, as the sun sank, and Kyle felt as if he were standing in the midst of a huge fire. Rynd's men danced in circles as someone began to beat on the drums. Kyle joined in the dancing, linking arms, swirling around and around and around, as they all, in unison, chanted ancient demonic melodies. Kyle could feel the energy and power building, escalating, more and more with each trip around the circle. He was descending into a trance-like state, and it was hypnotic.

As he entered his state, Kyle focused on summoning, from every far corner of the world, any and all dark powers that could aid his cause to kill Caitlin and Caleb. He visualized himself tearing Caitlin apart limb to limb, and he willed the universe to send him whatever assistance he needed. As the night grew thick, around and around he went, focusing, *willing* it to happen.

At some point in the night—Kyle didn't know how much time had passed—he finally opened his eyes, and found himself looking up at the sky. He noticed a lone figure descending, aiming right for the circle. Kyle broke away from the others, heading towards it, wondering what the universe had sent him.

He couldn't believe it. Standing there, facing him in the moonlight, was Sera. Kyle remembered her. She had been Caleb's wife. Yes, Kyle remembered with a smile. He had killed her son, Jade. The thought of it brought back fond memories. Kyle could not figure out what she was doing here. Had she come for vengeance?

He was surprised to see her standing there, so fearless, so full of rage. She reminded him of himself.

She took several steps towards him, standing but a few feet away.

"I've come to help your cause," Sera said.

Kyle looked back, skeptical.

"You and I share the same mission," she continued. "To destroy Caitlin and Caleb. To tear apart their union. I felt your energy. It summoned me here. I want to join your cause. Use me as you will, to exact your revenge. I have nothing else left to live for."

Kyle couldn't help but grin. As always, the universe had delivered to him exactly what he'd needed. Yes, he couldn't ask for anything more. A person Caleb trusted. She would be the perfect vehicle.

"Had do I know it's not a trick?" he asked. "After all, you were Caleb's wife."

Sera sneered.

"I'm *not* his wife. I despise Caleb. I have no time to waste, and no interest in tricking you."

Kyle surveyed her. She seemed honest; yet, still, it could be an elaborate trap.

"You might be a double agent," he responded. "Waiting to lure me in."

Sera seemed frustrated.

"How can I convince you?" she asked.

Kyle looked her over, and as he did, he suddenly admired her incredible physique. She was tall, nearly Kyle's height, wearing a skin-tight, black leather outfit, and she was curvy, with an amazing body, rippling with muscles. With long red hair, flowing down her back, matched by glowing green eyes, she was, Kyle thought, stunning. It had been a long time since he'd felt this way about another vampire, but as he stood there, he felt desire well up within him.

He realized exactly what she could do.

Yet, at the same time, Kyle wasn't stupid: he knew there was no possible way she could be attracted to him. With his missing eye, his burned face, his body covered with scars, he knew that he was grotesque looking to everyone. A monster. Especially to the female race. If Sera were willing to mate with him, that would prove it. Then he would know she was genuine.

And it would also give him the added satisfaction of mating with Caleb's one-time wife. And with the mother of the boy he killed.

Kyle grinned, an evil, lopsided grin.

"You will sleep with me tonight," he said. "During the festival, while the moon is at its height. My energy shall be yours, and yours mine. Then I will know that you are for real. Then you can join us, and we will destroy them both together."

Sera stared back at him with something like disgust. But she didn't flinch, or turn away. Instead, she stared, as if thinking.

"I could think of nothing that would hurt Caleb more," Sera said, staring Kyle up and down. And then she added: "And I could think of few better ways to exact my revenge."

To Kyle's surprise, Sera suddenly stepped forward and kissed him hard on the lips. She leaned back and stared into his eyes, and he could feel her energy, feel that she was just as aggressive as he was.

As Kyle felt her rage, her aggression, her ambition, he suddenly realized that he and Sera were perfectly matched. It was clear to him that they would both stop at nothing to get what they wanted.

He led her into the blackness, to a grassy plateau on the periphery of the torches. As the drums pounded all around them, as Rynd's men drank and danced and slaughtered and chanted, Kyle led Sera down to the ground, and he knew that this would be the beginning of a beautiful relationship.

CHAPTER TWENTY ONE

As Caitlin woke to the first rays of dawn streaming through her window, she felt an electric thrill to realize that this was her wedding day. She rose slowly from the comfort of bed, slipping out of the stack of warm furs, missing Caleb, his warmth beside her. They had followed the ancient vampire tradition, and had slept apart on this night before their wedding. She knew he was just down the hall, but it now felt strange to sleep in such a large bed alone, and she couldn't help missing him.

Caitlin gravitated to the castle window, looking out. It was the first day of November, the morning after Samhain, and the day was breaking cool and crisp. The leaves shimmered in a million vibrant colors, and the ever-present mist of Skye hung like a layer over everything. The dawn spread out in a soft, orange light, and it was magical: as it struck the mist, the entire island seemed as if it were covered in a rainbow.

"Mommy! It's your wedding day!" Scarlet exclaimed, running over and hugging her.

Caitlin looked down and smiled, and she could tell that Scarlet had been up for a while.

Ruth barked, and came limping over, licking Caitlin's hand. Caitlin was so happy and relieved to see Ruth up and walking around again, recovering well from her wounds. Caitlin had used her healing powers on her, and it had helped; but Ruth's wounds ran deep, and it would take time for her to recover fully. In fact, Caitlin didn't know if she would ever fully recover from her limp—and she suspected not. Still, to see her up and walking around lifted her heart.

"We're so excited!" Scarlet yelled. "Today you're going to be married to daddy!" she said, jumping up and down. Ruth barked again.

Caitlin felt a tremor of nervousness at the thought of the day before her, of how momentous it was. Her wedding day. It was really here.

Caitlin wasn't hung up on the details, on all the pomp and formalities; she just hoped that everything would go smoothly, without any drama. More than anything, she just wanted to be married to Caleb.

There was a knock on the door, and moments later, it opened and Taylor rushed in, followed by several of her bridesmaids, all carrying her exquisite wedding dress. Caitlin wondered for a moment where Polly was, assuming she would have been the first one to enter. But as the large oak door was still open, Caitlin suddenly spotted Polly across the hall, at the far end of it, exiting Sam's room. Caitlin smiled to herself, realizing that Polly had spent the night there. It made her feel good to think of her brother and Polly together. She thought they were the perfect match.

Polly rushed in and appeared with the others, her hair tasseled, looking sleepy, but eyes wide open, energetic, and looking more excited than she'd ever seen her.

"The day is here!" she yelled, barely able to contain her excitement, and the other girls cheered.

Within moments, Caitlin was lost in a whirlwind of girls enclosing her, dressing her, rubbing her with oils, doing her hair makeup, her hair, and a variety of things.

Suddenly, the door opened again, and an attendant appeared, holding out before him a small tray covered in a red velvet lining. Atop it sat the most beautiful necklace and earrings Caitlin had ever seen, sparking and shining with large diamonds, rubies and sapphires.

The girls, including Caitlin, all gasped.

The attendant smiled back, looking at Caitlin. "A gift from your husband-to-be on your wedding day."

There was dead silence in the room, as the girls all stared at the treasures. Polly reached over and took them, and came around behind Caitlin and put them on her. Caitlin was glad she had, because she would have been too intimidated to do so herself.

Caitlin now, more than ever, wished she was able to see herself in a mirror. But the awe-struck looks on the faces of all the girls, gaping at her, would have to suffice. Caitlin herself could see them shining as she looked down, and could feel their heavy weight in her ears, and around her neck, and she could feel how magnificent they were. She felt more indebted to Caleb than she ever had.

The girls rushed back to their preparations, and Caitlin told herself she just had to go with it. Caitlin felt as if it were all so surreal, as if she were lost in a dream. It would be, she realized, just the beginning of what would be a long, inexplicable, magical day.

*

The morning hours, immersed in getting dressed, in hair, makeup, all flew by in a rush. Caitlin wanted to slow it down, to savor every moment; but there was no way. This day seemed to progress faster than any day of her life.

Before Caitlin knew it, it was early afternoon, and she found herself being led to the periphery of the wedding aisle, concealed, with her bridesmaids, behind a laced-off waiting area. From her vantage point, she could see the long aisle, draped with a red carpet over the grass, leading to a gorgeous altar, covered in flowers. On either side of the aisle, to Caitlin's surprise, stood hundreds of vampires. Caitlin recalled being told that, in the ancient vampire tradition, vampires from fellow covens around the world would fly in to attend the ceremony and pay their respects.

In vampire tradition, nobody sat. Instead they all stood at attention, all dressed in the traditional vampire wedding garb—men wearing long-sleeved, velvet, black robes and women wearing the same, but in white. They all had a scarlet, linen cloth draped over their necks, like a necklace, hanging down low over the robe. The sight of so many people, so many of them strangers, made Caitlin more nervous.

Caitlin spotted Caleb, standing proudly at the end of the aisle, at the altar. Beside him stood Samuel, his brother and best man, and Caitlin was pleased to see them together. She knew that it meant the world to Caleb that Samuel had come. Polly, as maid of honor, would stand on the opposite side.

Caitlin was startled from her thoughts as Polly suddenly appeared, taking both her hands, and smiling broadly. Caitlin could see the love in her eyes.

"Are you ready?" Polly asked, excitedly.

Caitlin nodded, shaking inwardly, feeling too nervous to speak.

Polly hugged her tight, and Caitlin hugged her back.

"I love you," Polly whispered in her ear.

"I love you, too," Caitlin said, and meaning it. Polly now, more than ever, felt like a sister to her, the sister she'd never had.

Polly turned and signaled the bridesmaids, and they all began to filter out from behind the screen, each pairing up with a groomsmen and beginning to slowly walk down the aisle.

As they did, the music began. Caitlin looked over and saw a small chorus of four men and women, standing off to the side, singing an ancient Gregorian chant. It sounded beautiful, simple yet haunting. Timeless. Caitlin felt it was the perfect wedding song for this crowd.

Scarlet would be the last person to walk down the aisle before Caitlin. She stood there now, beside Caitlin, looking at her basket, which was overflowing with flowers, and which was attached to Ruth's collar. Scarlet had ingeniously devised a way to hang the basket to Ruth's neck, so that the two of them could walk down together, and Scarlet could reach in and throw the flowers that Ruth carried. Caitlin, happy to include Ruth hadn't objected.

Ruth looked excited to be part of it, but as Caitlin looked down, she saw that Scarlet now looked very nervous. Caitlin laid a reassuring hand on her head, and Scarlet smiled back.

As one song ended and another was beginning, Caitlin knew it was Scarlet's cue. She gently prodded her.

Scarlet regained her confidence, and began walking down the aisle. She reached over and grabbed flowers from the basket and threw them as she went. All the faces of the vampires lit up, as they watched her.

Now it was Caitlin's turn to feel nervous. Caitlin felt her heart pounding, as she knew it was her moment. She scanned the crowd once again for familiar faces, but saw very few. She had never met so many vampires at once, or had expected them all to turn out for her. She could tell from their smiles that they were there to wish her the best, yet still, it was a strange feeling.

As Caitlin began to walk slowly down the aisle, to the sound of the chants, she couldn't help but wish that she had someone to walk her down the aisle. A mother. A father. She had never been close with her mother, and actually wouldn't want her here. But her father—that was different. Of course, she felt closer to him now than she ever had, after all these lifetimes of searching for him, of receiving his clues, his letters—after his appearing to her in dreams and riddles. Now, more than ever, she wished that he was there, *really* there, holding her arm, walking her down. Not in a dream. Not as an apparition. But as a real, physical person.

Caitlin only hoped that one day he could really be there. That she'd really get to meet him. To spend time with him. That he could be a part of her life. And at that moment, for some reason, she suddenly wondered what he would think of her child. Of Scarlet. Of his grandchild. Would he be proud of her?

As Caitlin approached the altar, so dizzy from nervousness that she barely felt where she was going, she saw Caleb standing there, smiling back at her, and she felt at ease. He was dressed in the most beautiful attire she had ever seen, an outfit fit for a prince. It was a royal, black satin robe, with a high collar curving underneath his ears, a white shirt, and a scarlet tie. His hair was slicked back, formal, and he wore red gloves— apparently, another vampire tradition. He complemented his outfit with sparkling ruby cufflinks and shirt studs.

Over Caleb's shoulder, Caitlin saw Samuel, his brother, smiling back at her, and it felt good to see him again, after all these centuries. He looked the same, donning a beard and mustache, like an older, sterner, version of Caleb. On her other side, she turned and saw Sam, her brother, smiling back, too. Caitlin knew that behind her, on her side, were Polly, Taylor and the others. She felt comforted and reassured having all these people she loved up there with her.

And as she and Caleb turned and faced the man standing between them, she felt most comfortable of all. There, standing between them, presiding over the ceremony, was Aiden. He wore an all-white robe, his long silver beard protruding from beneath it. His expression was somber, intense. As always, his large blue eyes seemed to glow, staring back at them. But this time, his eyes were half-closed, and Caitlin could feel that he was focused, drawing down energy for this event.

The crowd stood absolutely still, waiting. The only sound Caitlin could hear was the cool November air whistling through. Finally, Aiden opened his eyes: they were a bright, shining blue, and they stared back at her with such intensity, that it nearly took Caitlin's breath away.

"We stand here today to witness the union of two beloved members of our race," Aiden began, in a deep, solemn voice. "I have known Caleb and Caitlin for many lifetimes. I can think of no two members more suited for each other. We have already seen the product of their union, and we wish on this day that the beautiful Scarlet may be the first of many more to come."

Aiden cleared his throat, and Caitlin and Caleb exchanged a furtive look, smiling.

"A vampire union is very sacred. It is not one to be taken lightly. It is forever. It is the definition of forever. It makes human love pale by comparison.

"Caitlin and Caleb have a love which is enduring. A love which has withstood many obstacles, many times, many places. It is a love I have rarely seen. It is a love which will transcend everything."

Aiden turned and looked at Caitlin.

"Caitlin, of the Pollepel Coven, do you hereby accept Caleb, of the White Coven, as your husband, to love and to cherish, for lifetime after lifetime? Do you vow to remain by his side, even though death shall never do you part?"

Caitlin turned and smiled at Caleb, and saw him smiling back. There was nothing she wanted more.

"I do," she said.

The crowd gasped. Aiden turned to Caleb.

"Caleb, of the White Coven, do you hereby accept Caitlin, of the Pollepel Coven, as your wife, to love and to cherish, for lifetime after lifetime? Do you vow to remain by her side, even though death shall never do you part?"

Caleb turned and smiled at Caitlin. "I do," he said.

Aiden reached out, took Caitlin's wrist in one hand, and took Caleb's in the other, and then held their palms up, until they were touching each other. He held them that way, and Caitlin could feel the energy coursing through his hand.

"The rings," Aiden prompted.

Caitlin reached into her pocket and extracted Caleb's wedding band. It was a magnificent ring, with a gold band, covered in sparkling rubies. It had been given to her as a gift by Aiden, and he had insisted that she give it to Caleb on his wedding day. As Caleb turned his hand, she reached out and placed it on his ring finger. It was the first time he'd seen it, and his eyes lit up with surprise and, clearly, admiration. It was a perfect fit, and Caitlin had never felt so proud.

Caleb, for his turn, reached in and extracted the most gorgeous wedding band Caitlin had ever seen, covered in diamonds and sapphires. Caitlin was shocked—she hadn't expected him to get her a second ring, above and beyond the magnificent ring she already wore. But as she looked down, he added this second ring to her finger, and Caitlin could immediately see how the two matched each other. She was speechless.

"By the authority vested in me," Aiden continued, "and by the authority of the grand vampire council, I, Aiden, of the Pollepel Coven, do hereby, through the thousand year tradition, pronounce you man and wife, vampire and vampire, merged together in a union that no man or vampire shall tear asunder."

He paused, looking at them both.

"You may kiss each other."

As they kissed, a cheer arose among the crowd. Joyful music broke out, to the sound of a lute and a harp, and vampires on both sides of the aisles threw handfuls of flower petals on them, as they turned and began to walk back down the aisle.

Caitlin felt the petals showering down, all around them, and broke into laughter, as did Caleb. Even while it was happening, Caitlin already knew that this was one of the peak moments of her life, one that she would never re-live again. She wished, more than anything, that she could just freeze it, hold onto it forever; but she knew, like everything else in the tide of life, it was something that could not last. So instead she just tried to enjoy it, staring at the petals, at Caleb's smile, feeling his love for her, and hoping that they could be together like this for eternity.

CHAPTER TWENTY TWO

Sam hadn't stopped dancing for hours. He could not remember a night in his life when he'd danced this long, or had a better time. He'd been drinking for hours, too, ever since the ceremony had ended, which had been followed by a feast to end all feasts.

There must have been thousands of torches placed around the ceremony and reception area, in the huge, open field before the castle. Even the castle itself was alight with torches, placed all around the moat, all along the entranceway, and even in every window. In fact, the moat itself was filled with ingenious floating candles.

As if all this were not enough, there were thousands of flowers, elaborate displays of every color, in every direction. There were huge vats of wine, even bigger vats of blood, and dozens of boars roasting on spits. These had been complemented by every sort of delicacy. Rounding out the festivities were dozens of musicians, jugglers, clowns, and all sorts of tournaments, games and fun. It had been a grand spectacle. And the night was still nowhere near over.

Sam couldn't be happier for his big sister, or his new brother in law. He was thrilled seeing the two of them so happy together. He was also elated for himself as he walked down the aisle with Polly, feeling how lucky he was to have her, and feeling her love for him as she held his arm. He couldn't help thinking, throughout the ceremony, of their night before, of how they'd spent the night in each other's arms, listening to the crashing of the waves. It had been a full moon, and they had slept right under it. Before dawn, he had taken her back to the castle, and they had slept in his bed.

For those precious few hours in which they'd slept in each other's arms, Sam had finally felt at peace in the universe. He was now certain, beyond a doubt, that Polly was The One.

Now, more than ever, he felt a desire to make the depth of his love known to her. Throughout the night, he'd felt an urgency to find her in the crowd, to express his feelings to her, and, inspired by his sister, to propose. But he hadn't been able to find her since the ceremony.

It had been a chaotic night, vampires streaming in from every direction, and it had been too hard to stick together. Vampires from every corner of the world grabbed him, danced, spun him around, and handed him off to partner after partner after partner. The music and dancing never stopped, and in the whirlwind, Sam had not been able to find her since.

Finally, he'd had enough, and had to catch his breath. He broke from the ranks and forced himself off to the side, to the wine vats, and he stood there, out of breath, combing the faces for her. He looked for her trademark hair, her large, bright eyes. But she was dressed like the others, and it was just too hard.

Suddenly, Sam felt a tapping on his shoulder.

Sam turned, and his heart soared.

Standing there, smiling back, her cheeks flush from dance and drink, was Polly.

She threw open her arms and gave him a big hug. He hugged her back, tightly, and spun her around.

She pulled back, and looked at him, and was beaming. He could see the love in her eyes.

"I missed you," Polly said.

"And I you," Sam said, and they came in for a long kiss.

"There's something I need to tell you," Sam said. "To ask you, actually."

Before she could respond, Sam took her hand and led her away from the crowd, off to the side. He desperately wanted time alone with her.

Sam found a quiet spot, away from the chaos, and as they stopped, he could see her looking back at him with surprise, unsure what it was.

"I want you to know that I meant what I said the other night," Sam began. "About...how much I love you."

Sam paused. He could feel his heart racing. He took a deep breath. He felt that now, more than ever, on the night of his sister's wedding, was the time.

Polly stared back, smiling, waiting.

"I want to be with you forever," Sam said finally.

"So do I," Polly said back.

Sam shook his head.

"No," Sam said. "I really mean it. *Truly.* Forever. Just like Caitlin and Caleb. *Forever.*"

Sam dropped to one knee, and took Polly's hand.

"I don't have a ring—yet," he said. "But I hope you won't hold that against me. I promise that when the time comes, I will get you the greatest ring you've ever seen."

Polly looked down at him, and broke into a smile.

"What are you asking me, Sam?"

Sam suddenly realized that, in his nervousness, he forgot to say the most important thing.

He smiled up at her.

"Polly?" he said, "will you marry me?"

Polly burst into a huge smile, and screamed. "YES!"

Sam stood, and Polly wrapped her arms around him in the tightest hug he'd ever felt. He lifted her, and spun her around, again and again, feeling his own joy in her response.

"YES YES YES!" Polly screamed. "A thousand times, yes!"

As Sam spun her around, again and again, he could feel her joy, her happiness coursing through him. And at that moment, he finally knew what true love was.

*

Caitlin looked up at Caleb as he held her in his arms, looking down at her with pure love. His eyes were shining with excitement, as he led her through the huge crowd, vampires cheering all around them. As Caleb parted the way through the crowd, leading them, Caitlin was overwhelmed. Her wedding night had been incredible, like a dream, from the ceremony to the feast, to the drinking, to the dancing....It was grander than any wedding she could have dreamed of.

On the one hand, the festivities never seemed to end, but on the other, the night went by in a flash. Caitlin couldn't believe it was already ending. And now, here she was, late into the night, holding Caleb's hand as he led her away.

Caleb led her through the cheering crowd, across the small drawbridge, over the moat, and through the grand castle entrance. He led her down the torch-lit, stone corridors, and up the winding, ancient stone staircase. As they reached the top, he picked her up, and carried her down the hall, past their room, and to the entrance of another room. Caitlin was surprised. She had never seen this room before. It was framed by huge, golden arched doors.

"The king has lent us his room for the night," Caleb announced with a grin, as he gently pushed open the doors with his shoulder.

Caleb carried her into the room, and as he did, she was awestruck at its opulence. It was unlike any other room in the castle, with huge, vaulted ceilings, several large windows, and an enormous four-poster bed, draped with furs, on top of which were strewn hundreds of rose petals. Petals also lined the floor, and candles were lit in every direction. Caleb closed the door behind them, carried Caitlin across the room, and placed her down gently in the bed.

The entire day and night had felt like a dream for Caitlin, and this was the perfect conclusion. She didn't know what she had done to deserve all this, to be so lucky. As she sank into the softest furs she had ever felt, she looked into Caleb's eyes, and wanted to hold onto this moment, onto him, forever. She didn't want anything to ever change. But even now, even on her wedding night, she knew that somehow it would. She tried desperately to push the thought out of her mind, to think only happy thoughts.

Caleb leaned in and kissed her, and she kissed him back.

"I love you with all my heart," Caleb whispered.

"I love you, too," Caitlin responded.

And she really meant it, with every pore of her body. She knew, after all they'd been through, that she'd finally found the one true love of her life, her destined partner, and that she would give anything to stay by his side forever. She thought back to her decision, lifetimes ago, on Pollepel, to go back in time and risk it all for him. She felt so grateful that she had done it.

As they rolled over in bed, Caleb leaned over and blew out the candles around them.

Now, finally, with all the obstacles behind them, all the ex-lovers, all the missions, all the misunderstandings, Caitlin finally felt confident—was determined—that nothing ever get between them again.

Yet somehow, deep inside, she couldn't shake the feeling that there was something ominous on the horizon, that their biggest trial was yet to come.

CHAPTER TWENTY THREE

Sera flew through the midnight sky, looking down on Caleb and Caitlin's wedding celebration. Down below, she saw hundreds of torches lighting up the night, hundreds of vampires gathered, drinking, dancing, celebrating. She watched it all with a burning rage.

In fact, Sera felt more rage than she usually did. Ever since she had mated with Kyle, ever since they had fed on each other and exchanged blood, Sera had felt different, infused with an entirely new energy. Her rage had multiplied to a level beyond which she'd ever known, and she found herself feeling angry about nearly everything. She could feel Kyle's energy and violence coursing through her, and she felt nearly out of control with hatred.

Sleeping with Kyle had been repulsive; it had been the last thing she had wanted to do. But she did what had to be done. It was more important to her now to get vengeance on

Caleb, and most of all, on Caitlin. Tearing their lives apart. That was what she lived for now.

If Sera couldn't have Caleb, then nobody could. Especially that pathetic creature Caitlin. To have to fly over and watch their celebration, watch their marriage, felt like a slap in the face. It felt as if they were spiting her, as if they were rubbing it in her face. Sera seethed with rage as she flapped her wings above all of them, taking it all in.

As Sera circled, she looked for any sign of the King. Kyle and Rynd had instructed her carefully, had told her all about King McCleod, about his weakness. He was a human with a penchant for vampires. He'd been in desperate search of a vampire to turn him, and this was, Rynd reasoned, the one weak point of the island: McCleod's desire.

They had dispatched Sera to go and find this McCleod, and to seduce him. Then, they could manipulate him, get him to do anything they wished—including ambushing Aiden's people with his human army.

Sera was happy to execute the mission, but she resented their thinking that she needed to offer him anything in order to seduce him. After all, she was Sera: gorgeous to vampires and humans alike. She could seduce anyone she wanted, anytime she wanted. She didn't need to offer them anything but herself.

And seduce this king, she would.

Finally, as Sera circled lower, she spotted the king. He was impossible to miss: he was seated at the head of a table, surrounded by followers, all obsequious in his presence. The huge fur mantle draped along his shoulders indicated it could be no one else.

Sera landed out of sight of the others, behind a grove of trees. She took position and watched McCleod carefully, observing how he drank, who he talked to. She was waiting for a vulnerable moment, when he wasn't surrounded by followers. She would catch him by surprise, and thus begin the seduction.

Sera's line of vision was occasionally blocked by dancers, then by musicians, and she felt like reaching out and tearing them apart. But she bit her lip, forcing herself to be disciplined, waiting patiently.

Finally, she saw her chance. McCleod rose from the table—everyone rising with him—and he gestured for them all to stay put, as he headed off himself towards a huge vat of wine. He stumbled just a bit as he went, and that suited her purposes perfectly.

Sera wasted no time. She sprinted across the field, around the side, and merged into the thick crowd, careful not to be noticed by anyone. She made her way to the vat of wine just before he did, just as she'd hoped.

She turned her back on him, pretending as if she were looking in the opposite direction, and blocked his path, so that he would have to get past her. She then casually reached over and held out an empty goblet of wine. She prided herself on being a student of human behavior, and having watched him, she could sense he had a chivalrous side. She could sense that he would do anything to help a damsel in distress. And she just knew that if she held out her goblet, he would want to help.

"Hand that to me," came the deep, royal voice.

Sera's back still to him, she smiled, realizing she had judged him perfectly.

Sera turned slowly, laying the full effect of her startling green eyes on him. She stared deeply into his, and offered the smallest hint of a smile. She tried to hypnotize him, using every vampire power of seduction she had.

It was working. She saw his eyes fix on hers, saw him forget to fill her goblet. And as she felt his fingertips touch hers, she realized that he had not let go. He looked like a deer caught in the headlights—and that was exactly what she wanted.

"I haven't seen you here before," he said.

Sera liked the sound of his voice: it was deep, confident, authoritative. Not like most humans.

"I'm new here," she said. She thought quick. "I've only come for the wedding."

Technically, it was not a lie. She had indeed come for the wedding—to tear it apart.

"Then we shall consider ourselves lucky to be graced by your presence," he said with a slight nod, then took her goblet, reached in, and filled it up.

He handed it back to her, and this time, as she took it, she laid her fingers on top of his, using her vampire power to send seductive energy into him.

As she slowly took the cup away, her fingers grazing his, she could see it was working.

"I've come from far away, and I'm only here for a short while," she said, in her most seductive voice. "I would be honored if you show me your castle before I go."

She waited and watched, her heart beating with anticipation. This was the moment, the crucial moment, when she would know. If he said yes, she knew that he would be hers.

"Surely, you have someone else to give you a tour of the grounds, aside from the King himself?" he asked with a smile.

She smiled back. "I have many. But none I want to accompany me. Except for you."

She waited and watched, staring deeply into his eyes. She could sense that he was still on the fence. This human was more confident, less impressionable, than the others. It was now or never.

She took a half step towards him, reached up and slowly let her open palm run down his chest.

"You're not of my kind, are you?" he asked.

She slowly shook her head. "No," she answered.

He stared for several more seconds, then finally, broke into a smile.

"Well, I guess I don't see the harm in taking a break from the party for a little while," he said, stepping forward and taking her arm. He turned and led her towards the castle.

Sera smiled as they walked, crossing the small foot bridge, over the moat, feeling victorious. As they approached the castle doors, the guards snapped to attention.

"What would you like to see first?" he asked, as they entered the grand hall, more guards snapping to attention.

She stopped and faced him boldly.

"Your bedchamber," she said.

She could see his eyes open wide in surprise, as he stared back at her.

"You are bold, aren't you?" he asked.

"As are you," she responded.

He stared at her, then suddenly turned and continued walking, leading her down another corridor.

They headed up a staircase, down several more corridors, guards snapping to attention all along the way, then finally towards a set of huge double doors. Two guards held it open for him, and as they walked through, they shut it behind them.

The room was magnificent, enormous, replete with a huge four-poster bed, rugs, candle chandeliers, and a roaring fire inside a marble mantelpiece. McCleod strutted in, then turned and faced her.

He stared at her with seriousness.

"Who are you exactly?" he demanded. "What is it that you want from me?"

Sera slowly raised her hand to his cheek.

"I want to give you something that you want," she said.

He stared back.

"I want to help you join my race."

McCleod's eyes opened wide.

"Why would you do such a thing? I have asked every vampire to turn me. They all refuse. Why are you different?"

Sera smiled, as she looked down and slowly unbuttoned his shirt, taking off the huge furs from his shoulders. She was happy to see that, while cautious, he was not resisting.

"Because I want something in return," she responded.

"And what is that?" he asked.

"I will tell you after I turn you. Whatever it is, you must vow to grant it to me."

He took a step back, and stared at her intently.

"You ask a high order," he responded. "I have no idea what it is you will want. It could be anything. It could be my kingdom. How can I vow to grant something when I don't even know what it is?"

She smiled back, prepared for this.

"Because what I'm going to give you is the greatest gift you could ever want. The gift of immortality. The gift of many lifetimes. You can lose a kingdom—that means nothing when you are immortal. You will have endless lifetimes to gain it back. Surely, you realize this yourself. Or else you would not want what we have? To be all-powerful. Is it worth honoring one small request?"

She could see he was wavering.

She stepped in, slowly rubbed her hands on his shoulders and removed his shirt. She led him closer to the fireplace. This time, he did not refuse.

"A full-fledged vampire?" he asked, breathing heavily. "Immortality?"

She leaned in, then placed her lips on his.

There was a brief moment when he paused, and she wasn't sure if he would give in.

But then, suddenly, he kissed her back, with full force, filled with a passion she had never anticipated. He picked her up into her arms and carried her to the pile of furs by the fireplace, and as he did, she knew that this night would change everything.

CHAPTER TWENTY FOUR

Caitlin walked through a field of torches. It was night, and the field was ablaze, a thousand spots of light flickering in the wind, as she walked down a meandering path. She was wearing her long, white wedding gown, and beside her, holding her arm, was her father.

She looked over at him, and he was smiling back. They walked down an endlessly long wedding aisle—but in place of a crowd on either side of them were flaming torches. At the end of the aisle, Caitlin could see, in the far distance, stood Caleb, at the altar, waiting.

There were so many questions Caitlin wanted to ask her father, so many things she wanted to say to him. But she didn't feel it was the right moment to speak, while he was walking her down. She could feel, though, how proud of her he was, and it made her feel good. She didn't want him to hand her off to Caleb— she didn't want him to ever leave—and she tried to slow their steps, to savor every moment.

Suddenly, she felt something, and looked back and saw that the trail of her dress had caught on fire. The fire crept slowly up the fabric, heading right for her.

Her father looked at her, still smiling, not noticing.

Caitlin tried to back away from it, frantic. "Daddy, please help me!" she screamed.

"Find me, Caitlin. You have to find me. There's just one key left. And then we will be together."

Caitlin felt the fire creeping closer to her, her whole dress a ball of flames. She could feel the heat, feel it about to scorch her skin. She knew that, in just moments, she would be burned alive.

"But I don't even know where to look!" she pleaded. "Please! Help me!"

"The Isle of the Celtic Saints," he said.

He suddenly turned, and held her shoulders firmly, and looked deep into her eyes. Somehow, she knew, that as long as he was holding her, the fire would be kept at bay.

"The Isle of the Celtic Saints," he repeated, more firmly.

Then, suddenly, he disappeared.

And as he did, the fire raged all around her. Caitlin threw her head back and screamed.

Caitlin sat upright in bed, screaming, swatting at the blankets around her, as if to put out a fire.

Caleb woke beside her, grabbing her shoulder.

"What's wrong?" he yelled. "What is it?"

Caitlin jumped up from bed, throwing the covers, looking all around her for any trace of fire. But there was none.

Still breathing hard, she slowly collected herself. It was just a dream, she realized. But it had seemed so real, so vivid. She felt as if her father were still in the room with her.

She turned and looked about the room, and saw that dawn was breaking, its first weak rays streaming through the castle window.

Her wedding night, she remembered. It was over now.

She looked around again, still disoriented, and realized she had spent the night with Caleb, and now it was over. It was already the next day.

"Caitlin?" Caleb asked.

But she needed time to think. She walked slowly to the window and looked outside, staring out at the landscape around the castle in the early morning sun, trying to collect her thoughts. It was getting harder and harder for her to tell the difference between dreams and reality these days; they almost seemed to blur into each other.

"Caitlin?" came Caleb's voice again, concerned as he crossed the room towards her.

There were just embers of a fire still burning in the fireplace, and Caitlin wrapped her hands over her bare shoulders in the cold, stone room, as she closed her eyes and tried to recall her dream. She saw her father. Heard his message. She felt certain that it was more than a message; it was a clue. The clue for where to go next.

She turned and faced Caleb, now only a few feet away.

"The Isle of the Celtic Saints," she said. "That's what my father said to me. He said to look for him there."

Caleb's eyes opened wide in surprise.

"Do you know it?" Caitlin asked.

He nodded. "Of course," he said. "I have heard of it. It is a very sacred place in the vampire world."

She looked at him, eager to know more.

"It must be a reference to the island of Eilean Donan. It was settled by the Celtic Saints in the sixth century. On it, there is a castle. An ancient fortification. Yes, it would make perfect sense. It is not far from here. And if there are any clues left to be found, I can think of no place more fitting."

"Then that is where we must go next," she said.

"Mommy? Daddy?"

They both turned to see Scarlet standing before them, dressed in her night robe, her hair tasseled, obviously having just woken up.

Scarlet ran into her arms, and Caitlin picked her up and hugged her.

"I had a bad dream," Scarlet said, over Caitlin's shoulder.

Caitlin could feel her crying.

"I dreamt that you died," she said. "I dreamt that you told me you were going away. You left me. And you never came back."

Caitlin felt her stomach drop. On all nights, her wedding night, for them both to have dreams filled with such darkness and premonitions. It didn't bode well, she thought.

But she tried to put it out of her mind. Instead, she looked over and exchanged a glance with Caleb. They were both thinking the same thing: Scarlet. When they embarked on their mission, what should they do with her? Of course, they couldn't bring her. Anywhere they were going, there was sure to be danger. And it would also slow them down if they needed to fight. It would be much safer for her to stay here, in the safety of the castle, in the safety of this kingdom, with Polly and Sam, all of Aiden's people, and all of the human warriors to watch over her. That was the responsible thing to do.

But Caitlin also didn't like her dream. Was it a bad omen? Scarlet clearly had deep powers, too, and Scarlet's dream did not give Caitlin the best feeling about leaving. Scarlet leaned back and stared into Caitlin's eyes, and Caitlin had the uncanny feeling that she was reading her mind.

"You would never leave me, would you?" Scarlet asked.

Caitlin swallowed.

"We would never leave you," Caleb began slowly, nervous. "You are our daughter, and we will be together forever, and nothing will ever change that. Do you understand?"

Scarlet nodded, wiping away her tears, seeming to feel better.

"We will always be together," Caitlin repeated, "but at the same time, sometimes Mommy and Daddy might need to go away for a few days. That doesn't mean we won't come back. We will always come back. But now is one of those times. We do need to go for just a few days—and then, I promise, we will be back."

"NO!" Scarlet screamed, bursting into tears as she hugged Caitlin. "I KNEW you would say that! You can't go! It's just like my dream. And now you're never going to come back!"

Scarlet was hysterical, inconsolable, as she sobbed in Caitlin's arms.

Caitlin turned and exchanged a look with Caleb. It was almost enough to give Caitlin pause, to make her wonder if they should change their plan, and bring Scarlet with them.

But Caleb, reading her mind, slowly shook his head, and she knew that he was right. They could not bring her with them. It would endanger them all. Caitlin sensed that wherever it was they were going, danger would not be far. After all, it was the final key they were after. The final key that would lead them to her father, the final key that would lead them to the ancient vampire shield. Who knew what adversaries might be awaiting them? It was hardly a mission suitable for a child.

Caitlin leaned back and looked Scarlet in the eyes, trying to get her to focus on her.

"I promise you, Scarlet," Caitlin said, over her cries, "that nothing bad will ever happen to you. Or to us. We will be back in just a few days. And then after that, we'll be with you all the time. You have to trust me. Do you trust me?"

Scarlet blinked, wiping away her tears, and finally, reluctantly, she nodded.

Scarlet seemed to calm a bit. But Caitlin, on the other hand, was feeling increasing foreboding. Indeed, for the first time in as long as she could remember, Caitlin wondered if they would, truly, make it back alive.

CHAPTER TWENTY FIVE

Sera awoke in the King's chamber at the crack of dawn. She threw open her eyes, immediately remembering the night before, and turned and stared at McCleod, naked, in bed beside her.

The two of them lay under the covers, she in his arms, and he sound asleep. That did not surprise her. She had seen this before: when people were first turned, they often slept long and late—sometimes for days. And this had been an epic turning. They had been together all night long, and she had never met a more willing human victim.

Sera jumped out of bed in a single bound, needing to clear her head from the night before. The body warmth from the sheets immediately evaporated, leaving her cool in the November morning, and she grabbed a silk robe and put it on as she made her way to the windowsill. She looked out at the first crack of dawn, the blood red sun on the horizon, and felt it was a good omen. She contemplated her next move.

So far, all had gone according to plan: soon McCleod would be one of hers, of her kind, and he would be putty in her hands. He had vowed to do as she wished, and she would call in the vow. Then, finally, they could execute their plan. Kyle and Rynd had been smart to come up with this: the vampires here would never expect an attack from within their own island, a human attack from within their own ranks. What she would demand of McCleod would be the ultimate treachery: he would rally his human warriors, with all their silver-tip weapons, surround Aiden's people, and catch them by surprise. If all went as planned, Aiden's entire coven would be wiped out by nightfall. Along, of course, with Caitlin and Caleb.

McCleod would provide a crucial attack on one front. And Kyle and Rynd, at the same time, would attack on another, using their own treachery. With this two-front war, there was no way any of them could escape.

Sera smiled at the thought of it. Finally, she would have vengeance. She would spend hours torturing Caitlin. And then she would make Caleb be hers again—right before she killed him. *No one* crossed her.

"Leaving so soon?" came a dark voice.

Sera wheeled, startled.

She was shocked. Standing just inches away was McCleod. He was awake. Already. And judging from the vicious look in his now-red eyes, he was fully turned. Somehow, he had managed to cross the room without making a single noise.

Sera had underestimated him. His recovery was quicker than she could have imagined, and he was more nimble on his feet than she would have guessed. She had created a far more powerful vampire than she could have ever predicted. She was at a loss for words.

He smiled back. "You did your job well," he said.

He lifted his arm and stared at it in awe, slowly squeezing open and shut his fist, admiring his newfound power.

"I've never felt such power in my life. Despite years of training, years of sparring. I've never felt this quick, this nimble. I feel a thousand times the strength I've ever had." He looked around. "In this room, even in this dim light, I can see so much better. Sharper."

He turned and faced her, his eyes darkening as they locked onto hers.

"I vowed something last night. I owe you something. What is it?" he demanded. "Tell me now, so I can move on with my life. I have wars to wage, kingdoms to conquer."

Sera smiled back, admiring his pugnaciousness.

"But you can't conquer anything until you first give me what I want," she reminded, enjoying having him in her power.

He frowned back.

"And what if I don't? You can't stop me. I am a vampire now, as powerful as you."

"Perhaps you are," Sera retorted, "but I can summon an army of vampires to destroy you in an instant. You can't run or hide from all of us."

He stared back at her, and slowly, he seemed to soften, to become slightly less arrogant.

"Then I ask again: what is it you want?"

Sera smiled, relishing the moment. Now she had him exactly where she wanted him.

"Just one small favor, one tiny task. In fact, it is amazing how small it is, given what I just did for you. It will take you but a day, and then you'll be out of my debt forever."

He stared back impatiently.

"You are going to summon your army of human warriors," Sera continued. "Everyone in your kingdom, all your best warriors, all who carry silver-tip weapons. All those who are closest to Aiden's people."

"And?" he snapped, impatient. "And then what?"

Sera smiled.

"You will order them to attack and kill all of Aiden's men."

McCleod gasped, speechless. His frown turned into a scowl.

"I would never do such a thing," he said, outraged. "Aiden trusts me. And I him. We are brothers, warriors-in-arms. They have always been good to me, and I to them. I would never harm them, would never break the warrior code. I will not do it. But ask for something else, and that you shall have."

Now it was Sera's turn to scowl.

"I only ask once—and I shall have whatever that thing is. You vowed. You cannot go back."

McCleod suddenly turned and stormed away, heading for the door.

Sera felt all the fury rise through her, the fury and strength not only of her, but also of Kyle, his blood now coursing through her veins. She felt stronger and more powerful than she ever had—and in a deeper rage than she knew possible.

In a single leap, she crossed the room, grabbed McCleod from behind, and slammed him down to the floor, pinning him in a deadly lock.

He squirmed beneath her, but he was unable to move an inch. Clearly, Sera, was far more powerful.

"You've been a vampire for a day," Sera scowled, "while I have been one for millennia. In the vampire world, strength does not go by gender. It goes by age. And I'm far, far stronger than you will ever be."

He finally stopped struggling, clearly defeated, broken.

"You will do what I wish of you."

"I will," he answered, barely getting the words out.

"You will kill Aiden's people. Repeat it after me."

"I will kill Aiden's people," he repeated, grunting, struggling to breath.

Sera smiled. Finally, she would have her revenge.

CHAPTER TWENTY SIX

Caitlin and Caleb flew through the early morning over the Isle of Skye, heading east for the mainland of Scotland, right into the sun. As they flew, Caitlin looked down, and took in the extraordinary beauty of the Isle of Skye. It was one of the most magical places she had ever seen. The ever-present mist hung over everything, and beneath it, she could see the hills and valleys, the green moss covering everything, the thousands of small lakes interspersing the landscape. All along the island's perimeter were high, sharp cliffs, dropping hundreds of feet down to the ocean, and the beautiful foam of the waves crashing against the shore. The island was so remote, untouched, with no roads to speak of. It was truly a place for the brave.

Caitlin's thoughts turned to Scarlet's dream, her premonition that she would not return. Despite herself, Caitlin could not help feeling herself that Scarlet was right, that she would not return to this place. She knew it was crazy, but she took one long look at the island as if it would be her last. She had a persistent sense of foreboding and dread that she'd been unable to shake.

Leaving Scarlet behind had been hard. She had woken Polly, had deposited Scarlet and Ruth with them, and had made them promise to guard them with their lives. They had, and that had set Caitlin somewhat at ease. Caitlin knew there was nothing she should be worried about: surely Sam and Polly would never leave Scarlet unprotected—especially after they had messed up in England. Not to mention, Scarlet was also in the safety of the castle, with Aiden's men, and the King's men, all around to protect her. Caitlin could not understand why she was so concerned.

As they flew over the strip of ocean separating the Isle of Skye from the mainland of Scotland, Caitlin, holding Caleb's hand, reflected on the day and night before. Her wedding. The ceremony. The reception. Her night with Caleb. Her dream. This morning….So much had happened so quickly.

As it was the morning after her wedding, she realized that this would be the traditional time for their honeymoon. And in a way, oddly, it was: the two of them were leaving, traveling, going on an adventure, just the two of them. And surely, wherever they went, they would be romantic places, a castle or a church, or some other ancient site. So in a way, this was an odd sort of honeymoon.

But in another way, their mission now had a much more serious and urgent feel to it. Ever since her dream, Caitlin felt the ticking of time, felt an urgency to find the fourth key, and to return to Scarlet. Caitlin's heart pounded at the thought of what she might find. Would her father be there, waiting in Eilean Donan? Would the mission finally be finished? And if so, would it change her life forever? Would she be sent back to the future? Or back further into the past?

The morning sun rose high in the sky as they flew and flew. Eventually, they were over land again. Caitlin looked down and saw that the land here, in the Highlands of Scotland, was just as beautiful as it had been in Skye. Caleb held her hand and dived lower, and in the distance, Caitlin could already see the outline of where they were going.

It was impossible to miss. Eilean Donan. Even from here, from this great distance, Caitlin could see it was one of them most romantic and beautiful castles she had ever seen.

Caitlin reached down and felt her pocket and clutched the clue, the ancient, torn page that McCleod had given her, now rolled up in a scroll. As they approach the castle, she felt it throbbing in her hand, and she wondered if this place would yield the answer, provide the second half of the clue that could lead to the final key.

"Eilean Donan is a very sacred place," Caleb said over the wind, as they dove lower, circling it. "It has been home to vampires for thousands of years. The last I heard, it was home to the Red Coven. A very powerful and deadly coven, often inhospitable to outsiders—and rumored to be the guardians of a deep secret."

They dove lower, and Caitlin took in the site of the castle from all sides. It was even more impressive up close. Built on a small island in the middle of a lake, Eilean Donan castle was accessible only by a long, stone footbridge, suspended over three small arches. The castle was set against green, rolling hills on every side, mountains in the distance, and the vast expanse of the lake surrounding it. It was a dramatic and romantic landscape, and the castle, already looking ancient, with parapets on multiple levels, blended perfectly into the countryside. A gentle mist hung over the lake, lit up in the sun, adding to the romance of it. Caitlin could already sense that it was a mysterious place, and that it held ancient secrets.

They circled again and again, debating where to land. Caitlin spotted dozens of vampire guards stationed, all dressed in long, blood-red cloaks. She wondered if they would have to battle them, but wanted to avoid a confrontation if they could.

"Let's let them know we're friendly," Caitlin called out. "Let's land by the main gate."

"But if they confront us, better to land on the roof," Caleb responded.

"I don't feel that they will confront us," Caitlin said. "If they are guardians of the vampire secret, I think they will appreciate why we are here. They might even be expecting us."

Caleb looked skeptical, but he agreed, and together they dove down, right for the main gate.

Moments later, they were standing at the end of the footbridge, before the main castle gate, in a wide open plaza guarded by dozens of vampires.

The vampires, dressed in red, scowled back, and Caitlin hoped that she had made the right decision.

As she took several steps forward, towards the entrance, suddenly, the main castle gate opened, the heavy iron spikes slowly rising. A single vampire approached, standing out from the others as he was the only one dressed in all white. He had a long beard spilling out from under it, and as he approached, he pulled back his hood and stared at them both with an intense stare. He was followed by a dozen guards, and Caitlin briefly wondered if they were about to attack.

But then she saw the lead vampire break into a smile, and finally, she felt at ease.

"Caitlin and Caleb," he said slowly, shaking his head. "I've heard a lot about you two. I am honored you've come to our remote corner of the world."

With that, he suddenly turned and walked into the castle.

Caitlin and Caleb looked at each other, and figured there was only one thing to do: to follow him.

*

"Most vampires who come here, come looking for the Grail," the lead vampire said, as they walked through an ancient stone corridor. He turned to them and smiled. "But I can tell that you two are different. You are looking for something else, something much more sacred."

"I'm looking for my father," Caitlin replied.

"Yes, I know you are," the vampire responded. He stopped and faced her. "I knew him well. He was an amazing man."

Caitlin's heart raced.

"Is he here?" she asked, excitedly.

He laughed, a short, little sound. "I wish he was. No, I'm afraid he hasn't been here for centuries. But he left a very important legacy here. And he prepared us for your arrival. Centuries ago."

The man turned, opened a small, medieval door, and they all headed down a new corridor, twisting and turning.

"What did he prepare?" Caitlin asked, burning with curiosity.

The man stopped before another door. "There was something he wanted you to have. You and only you."

He opened another small door, and Caitlin had to duck as she walked through the opening.

This door opened into a grand room, lit by dozens of torches, with high arched ceilings, and stained-glass. It looked like a chapel, and at the end was a large, shining gold altar, guarded by two vampire soldiers, dressed in red, who stood at attention. Caitlin wondered what could be so valuable and precious that two guards would have to stand watch over it at all times. She wondered if it was the second half of the torn page.

As they approached it, her turned to her, "Your clue?" the vampire prodded.

Caitlin wondered for a moment what he was asking for, then realized it must have been the torn page. She reached in and extracted it.

He slowly shook his head.

"That is not for this place," he said. "Your necklace," he corrected.

Caitlin momentarily forgot what he was referring to; then she reached down and removed her small antique cross, grateful once again that she still wore it.

The man gestured towards an ancient, bejeweled chest, and Caitlin knelt down, and inserted her cross with the click. She turned it, and it slowly opened.

She could not believe what she saw.

CHAPTER TWENTY SEVEN

Polly awoke from a night of exquisite dreams, happier than she had ever been. She had been riding on cloud nine ever since Sam had proposed to her the night before. She had been secretly, deep down, hoping that he would, especially on Caitlin and Caleb's wedding night. She knew that she had no real reason to expect this, given that they had barely been together a few days—and yet somehow, deep down, she still hoped for it anyway. She had never loved anyone as much as Sam, and she'd wanted him to propose to her more than anything.

Polly had gone to bed ecstatic and had dreamt all night long that she and Sam had been walking through a field of white flowers, white rose petals showering all around them, as the sun never seemed to set. She saw the two of them walking into the white light, and she awoke with the most peaceful feeling of her life, feeling so relaxed and content. She'd had the strangest, fleeting thought, that, given how happy and content she was, she'd be perfectly happy to die right now, on this day. After all, there was nothing more she could ever want from the world.

After laying with her in bed most of the morning, Sam had finally arisen, seeming as happy as she was. He'd said he wanted to celebrate, to go out and hunt for them, to find the biggest, wild boar he could, kill it, and bring it back for a special feast for them two of them that night. It was to be a celebration of their love, he'd said. And he wanted to find the perfect animal himself.

Polly loved the idea. She could use the day, herself, to get ready and prepare all the vegetables that could go with it. It would be like their own special wedding night.

Polly gave him a long kiss goodbye, knowing she would see him in just a few hours. Yet deep down, she had the craziest feeling that she might not. She didn't understand the feeling at all—it made no rational sense. Still, as Sam turned to walk out the door, she reached out, grabbed his wrist, and pulled him back to her, and hugged him tight. She did not let go for several seconds.

"What is it?" Sam asked, surprised, looking down with concern.

Polly slowly shook her head and forced a smile, knowing she was just being crazy.

"Nothing," she said. "I just love you."

Sam leaned in and kissed her, and then turned and walked out the door.

That was when Polly felt it. Her first pang.

It struck her so hard in the stomach, she keeled over from the unfamiliar sensation, having no idea what it was. Just as she tried to stand, it hit her again.

And again.

Finally, Polly realized that something was wrong. She sat on the edge of her bed, in a sweat, wondering what on earth it could be. After several more pangs, she had the craziest idea. Could it be possible that she was pregnant?

She knew that two vampires could not get pregnant. But then again, Sam was no ordinary vampire. And neither was she. She also knew that vampire pregnancies manifested quickly, usually within 48 hours. Could it be possible?

Polly quickly ruffled through her drawers, and finally found the ancient locket her great-great-grandmother had passed onto her. She remembered her words, from centuries ago: *if a vampire is pregnant, then her reflection will show once—just once—in this ancient mirror. If you see yourself, for the first and only time, that is how you will know.*

Polly wiped the dust off the heavy, silver locket and slowly opened it, her heart pounding. Part of her knew she was being ridiculous, given how unlikely it was. But another part of her *had* to know.

Polly looked down and stared into the mirror.

She saw herself, staring back, with a startled expression. It was such a shock to see her own image in the mirror—she never had before—and at the same time, her heart raced to know that it was really true. She was pregnant.

Another pang suddenly struck her, but this time, Polly jumped up in joy, screaming, ecstatic. *Pregnant.* Her. With Sam's child.

She didn't think she could be any happier—but now, her joy tripled. She couldn't wait until she told Sam the news. He would probably keel over in shock.

And Caitlin. She had to tell her. And all the others.

No. She had to tell Sam first. And he wouldn't be home for hours. Now, those hours felt like an eternity.

Pregnant. Her!

She shouted again in joy, hardly believing it. She would have to keep this a secret, at least until tonight. But how could she!? Keeping a secret was the hardest thing for her—and this was the secret to end all secrets.

Polly got excited thinking of seeing Sam tonight. She would spring the news on him over dinner. She would dress for the night in her nicest fineries, wear the nicest oils, and surprise him. She thought of the most beautiful dress she owned—an all-white, silk dress—and suddenly realized it needed to be washed. She ran to her closet and pulled it out, examining it, then grabbed her washing wrack and soap, preparing to head down to the lake.

Suddenly, the door opened, and in marched Scarlet and Ruth. And then Polly remembered: earlier that morning, while she was half asleep, Caitlin had woken her and made her vow to watch over Scarlet carefully while she took off on her mission. Polly, of course, had been thrilled to agree. She loved Scarlet, and, after all, there wasn't much to do: those two could hardly be more safe than within these castle walls, the most heavily guarded compound Polly had ever been in. Polly would hardly need to do a thing, except entertain them for a few days.

Polly was bursting with excitement, and was dying to tell Scarlet the news. But at the last moment, she stopped herself, holding her tongue, knowing she should tell Sam first.

But as she looked down, she noticed tears in Scarlet's eyes, and was suddenly concerned.

"What is it, love?" Polly asked, kneeling down and wiping a tear off her cheek.

Scarlet started to cry. "Mommy and Daddy left me."

"Oh sweetheart, they didn't leave you. They only went away for a day or two. They'll be back before you know it. In the meantime, you have me. Right?"

Scarlet nodded.

"And we're going to do all sorts of fun things together. You and me, and Ruth and Sam. It's going to be like one long party." She put on a big smile. "Okay?"

Scarlet slowly nodded, wiping away her tears.

"Now I just need to run down to the lake for a minute to wash these clothes. I'll be back within the hour. You and Ruth just sit tight, and I'll be back before you know it. Just stay inside the castle, okay?"

"No!" Scarlet snapped back, suddenly fierce.

Polly was taken aback by the strength and authority in her voice. For a moment, she felt as if she were talking to an adult warrior. She wondered where that power came from, and wondered what other powers this child carried.

"I'm *not* staying here!" Scarlet yelled. "I'm going with you! I'm not going to leave your side. And neither is Ruth."

Polly was stunned. She didn't quite know what to say. She had never seen Scarlet act this way before. She didn't like the idea of their coming to the lake. Not that there was anything to worry about; but still, she had promised Caitlin. And the safest place in the world was right here, in this castle.

"I'm sorry, sweetheart," Polly said, more firmly "but I made a promise to your Mommy and Daddy, and you need to stay here. You must stay inside the castle, where it's safe. But I'll be back within the hour, okay?"

"No you won't," Scarlet said to her, matter of factly. "I've already seen your future. You'll be dead within the hour," she pronounced.

An icy chill ran up Polly's back, and her hairs stood on end. It was the most terrifying thing anyone had ever said to her. And coming from Scarlet, it was so authentic, stated as if it had already happened. It took Polly's breath away, and she had no idea how to even respond.

But she didn't have a chance. Suddenly, Scarlet turned and strode away from her, with Ruth, out the door, and slammed it behind her. The walls shook, and as they did, Polly couldn't help feeling as if her fate had just been sealed.

CHAPTER TWENTY EIGHT

As Polly headed down the hill to the lake, clutching her white, silk dress, she felt a terrible foreboding. Scarlet's words still lingered with her, and Polly marveled at how such a young child could speak with such authority. Polly had a creepy, ominous feeling that would not go away; she looked over her shoulder at the castle, for good measure, and wondered briefly if she should turn back.

But she realized she was being ridiculous. Legions of Aiden's warriors, and of the King's warriors, stood guard in every direction. She looked back at the lake, and saw nothing but clear skies and open water. They were in a remote place, heavily fortified, hundreds of miles from any possible harm. And Sam would be back in just a few hours. Everything looked absolutely normal, and there was no sign of danger anywhere in sight. Besides, she had a dress which needed washing, and it wouldn't take very long.

Polly turned and continued down the gently sloping hill, towards the lake. As she did, the sky darkened with thick clouds, and a cold wind picked up, brushing her face. She took a deep breath, and finally forced herself to dismiss it all as just the ramblings of a precocious young child, one overwrought that her parents had just left. Of course, children could imagine things, and Scarlet was no exception. Polly forced herself to conclude that the whole thing was ridiculous, and to focus on quickly washing her dress and returning to prepare for Sam's arrival.

Polly brightened at the thought of it, as she reached the lake. She knelt at its shore and began scrubbing her dress in the icy water. As she did, another cold wind picked up, this one stronger than the last, rippling the water and the otherwise still lake, forcing Polly to take a break and look up.

Polly was surprised. Seemingly out of nowhere, there appeared a small canoe on the water, drifting her way, and quickly. Polly looked at it, puzzled. Where had it come from? How had it gotten so close so fast?

She was even more taken aback as she saw a head rise up out of the canoe. It was the head of a man who was injured, his face covered in blood, and he looked right at Polly, and held out a hand for her help.

Polly stood, her heart suddenly pounding. It was a face she would recognize anywhere in the world.

It was Sam.

Polly ran out into the water, not even feeling the ice cold pain rippling through her calves as she ran up to her thighs, grabbed the canoe, and pulled it close.

There was no mistake about it: it was Sam, lying on his back, covered in blood. How was it possible?

"Help me, Polly," he said, weakly.

It was the strangest thing she had ever experienced. It was definitely Sam, down to the last iota. It was his hair and clothes and body and voice. It was *definitely* him.

But at the same time, there was something that Polly sensed, somewhere deep inside, that told her it was not Sam. She couldn't understand it.

"What happened?" Polly yelled out to him, frantic that he was hurt.

"Please, help me," he said, reaching out a hand.

She grabbed it. It was icy cold, and left blood on her wrist. She pulled him close to her, and felt herself wanting to break into tears. But she forced herself to be strong for him. She couldn't imagine what might have happened to him.

"What happened to you?" she yelled out. "How can I help? What can I do?"

"Can I come onto the island?" he asked, weakly.

"What kind of question is that?" she asked, confused. "Of course you can," she replied, as she went to pick him up in her arms.

But he resisted, staring fiercely back at her.

"So are you inviting me?" he pressed. "Do you invite me onto the island?"

Polly stared back at him, narrowing her eyes, unsure what he was talking about. Was he delusional? Had he been injured in the head? Was he not thinking clearly?

"What do you mean, do I invite you?" she asked. "Why would you need an invitation?"

"Answer me," he said, clutching her wrist. "Please," he added, softening. "I need your help. Will you invite me?"

"Of course I invite you. You are invited. There. Are you happy? Now stop talking crazy, and let me help you," she said, and swooped down and picked him up in her arms. She turned and carried him to shore.

This time, he did not resist. Polly couldn't help thinking how peculiar it was, his wanting to be invited. She couldn't even comprehend what he meant by it. He must be delusional.

She tried not to think of it, as she carried him through the water, and onto the shore. She lay him down gently on the sand and knelt beside him, ready to tend his wounds.

More than anything, she was bursting to tell him the news. About their child. But she knew this was the wrong time. So instead, she checked his body, trying to find the source of his injury.

But oddly, she could not find anything. As she examined him, he seemed perfectly fine.

She suddenly sat up and reached into his waistband. She wondered what he was reaching for, and then, in the sudden afternoon light, she saw something gleaming. A weapon.

A knife.

Before Polly could open her mouth to ask him what he was doing, suddenly, Sam reached the knife up high, and plunged it into her heart.

It was a silver knife, Polly saw, right before it entered her. She felt it plunge into her chest, right into her heart.

Polly was too shocked to scream. Instead, she sucked in her breath, gasping for air, staring at Sam with more surprise and horror than she'd ever thought possible.

She could feel the life ebbing out of her, out of her child yet unborn. She looked into Sam's eyes and saw him staring remorselessly back— and her final thought, before her world turned black, was how much she had loved him.

CHAPTER TWENTY NINE

Scarlet stormed out of the castle, Ruth by her side, and marched over the footbridge, determined to track down Polly and make sure she was safe. Scarlet had been sure about her premonition. With each passing day, she felt her powers grow stronger, felt herself able to see more clearly into the future—and she knew she was right. In fact, she had brought her bow and arrow with her, had snatched it off the training ground, along with a small quiver of arrows. Scarlet felt confident in her own skill as an archer, reinforced by everyone's praise on the training grounds, and she felt that she could be of help in protecting Polly from whatever it was that was coming for her.

Besides, Scarlet did not like taking orders from anybody, or just sitting around the castle, confined—especially when she felt something bad might happen to others. And she wasn't afraid. In fact, she *never* felt afraid. The only thing she felt afraid of was not being allowed to take action of her own.

Scarlet jogged down the grassy hill, and as she got closer to the lake, her sense of foreboding increased, and she broke into a sprint. Ruth, beside her, was on edge, too, her hair standing up on her back, and her fangs revealed. Ruth, too, must have sensed it.

As they rounded the hill and the view unfolded before them, Scarlet saw that she had been right. She couldn't understand what she saw: there was Sam, standing over Polly, reaching up a knife, and getting ready to plunge it down.

Scarlet screamed.

But it was too late. Before her words got out, before she could react, the knife was already descending, plunging towards Polly's heart. Scarlet felt her breath taken away as she watched the horrific sight. She couldn't understand why Sam would ever do such a thing.

But then, as she watched, right before her eyes, Sam's face transfigured, morphed into someone else. He was now a disgusting man, with a square jaw, a pockmarked face, and large, black eyes. It hadn't been Sam after all. It had been someone else, some evil creature who had pretended to be Sam. A shapeshifter.

Behind this man, suddenly, the water blackened with hundreds of boats, all containing vampires, and then the sky, too, blackened with hundreds more vampires. It looked like an entire vampire army, all waging war, and all heading right for the Isle of Skye. Scarlet couldn't believe it. It was as if this first person had somehow led the way for an entire vampire army.

But Scarlet wasn't about to run. On the contrary. She wanted vengeance for Polly. So instead of turning around, Scarlet ran forward, right for her attacker. And Ruth ran right beside her.

Scarlet ran until she was about twenty yards away from him, just as her attacker was standing, rising to his full height. With no time to lose, she quickly took a knee, pulled back her bow, inserted an arrow, and took steady aim. She aimed for his left eye.

He saw her, but before he could react, she had already let the arrow fly.

It was a perfect hit. It went right into his eye, knocking it out clean. The arrow lodged in his head, and the man shrieked in agony, grabbing at it, trying to pull it out. Scarlet was shocked at what she had managed to do: she only wished it had been a silver-tipped arrow, and had killed him on the spot.

But the man didn't die, or didn't even collapse. Instead, she watched in horror as the man reached up and yanked the arrow right out of his skull. He threw it to the ground, and, with one eye socket bleeding, scowled directly at her.

He broke into a sprint, heading right for her, just as the sky was blackening with a swarm of vampires, getting closer. Scarlet knew, at that moment, that she and Ruth were finished. There was no point in her even trying to run, because she knew she wouldn't make it. So instead, she stood her ground bravely, chest and chin up, waiting to face her attacker head on.

Scarlet suddenly felt hands around her, and the next thing she knew, she was being picked up by someone from behind, lifted up into the air. The person picked her up with one arm, and picked up Ruth in the other. The person was the fastest she had ever seen, and in the blink of an eye, Scarlet and Ruth were soaring in the air, being whisked away from the vampires chasing them.

Only after they were a good distance away, did Scarlet summon the courage to look up and see who it was who was carrying them, who had saved them from sure death.

She breathed a breath of relief as she recognized him.

It was the man from the beach, the man who was in love with her Mommy.

It was Blake.

CHAPTER THIRTY

Sam had been having one of the best days of his life. He had been riding on cloud nine since the night before, enjoying himself every minute of his big sister's wedding. He was so happy for Caitlin and Caleb, and so overjoyed that their wedding had been such a success. Finally, after all the obstacles between those two, Sam was ecstatic to see them together, permanently. It brought a sense of relief to him, as it also made him feel there was now someone else in Caitlin's life to watch over and protect her.

As if all that had not been enough, it had also been the most incredible night of his life with Polly. He kept reliving the moment in his head, again and again, when he'd asked her to marry him. Her expression. Her response. Her hugging him. He had felt her joy coursing through him, in every pore of his body, and at that moment, he had never felt so right in the world. He knew he had made the perfect decision, and was so looking forward to spending the rest of his life with her.

Sam had awoken this morning with a new bounce in his step. He was determined to celebrate his engagement to Polly, to formally announce the news to everyone later that day, and to make this a beautiful day and night for her. Now, it was their turn.

Sam decided that he'd make it really special: he would go out and hunt himself, personally, for the biggest and fiercest boar he could find. He would bring it back, and they would celebrate with a feast, and a night of drinking and games.

And now, here he was, relaxed and refreshed. He had spent the morning alone, out in the woods, hunting. The hours alone outdoors had provided him a sense of tranquility, and had allowed him time to process everything from the night before, and to enjoy it all again. It had grounded him. He enjoyed quietly tracking and listening for game.

After hours of searching, of walking quietly, deep in the woods, Sam suddenly heard a twig snap. He stood perfectly still, and a moment later, the biggest and fiercest boar he had ever seen, its tusks sharp and curled a foot-long, charged right for him. Sam relished the battle.

He waited, then, using his vampire skills, leapt over it at the last second. The boar turned and charged again, and this time, Sam stepped to the side, dodging it, enjoying the sport, taking his time before killing it.

The boar was enraged. It charged Sam again, and this time, Sam jumped on its back, reached down, and prepared to snap its neck.

But it did something which caught him by surprise: the animal managed to spin its head around, and to gorge Sam with its tusk, slicing his arm. Sam, shocked, cried out in pain. He was stunned. Ever since he had become a vampire, no animal had ever managed to put the slightest scratch on him. Nothing could ever come close to matching his speed or strength. Sam, furious, quickly snapped its neck, and the two of them went tumbling to the ground, the boar dead.

But Sam was shaken. He didn't understand what had just happened, how it was possible. How could he be even the slightest bit vulnerable?

Thinking it over, he realized that what had just happened was impossible. It must have been a supernatural occurrence. It was the universe, sending him a sign. An omen. But of what?

Sam didn't like it. It gave him an ominous feeling, a sense of foreboding. He felt as if the universe were hinting that something terrible was happening somewhere. Sam stared at the huge animal, lying there on its side in the grass, dead, and he no longer wanted to bring it back. It felt to him like a reminder of a bad omen.

Sam left it where it was. He slowly backed away from it, wondering.

The sky suddenly darkened, thick clouds gathering on the horizon, and Sam felt a cold breeze brush his face. He turned and headed back down the path, feeling it was time to return.

The more Sam walked, the more he felt it: something was wrong. Worse, he began to feel that something was wrong with Polly. Danger.

Sam broke into at a sprint, then leapt into the air, flying for all he was worth. He broke out of the woods and into open sky, and the more he flew, the more his senses screamed to him that something was very, very wrong. It was like a beacon, calling to him. It practically screamed at him to hurry to the lake.

Sam flew even faster, faster than he even knew was possible, tucking his wings in, diving through the air, until moments later, he was circling over the lake. The lake was still, and as Sam circled it, at first he saw nothing wrong.

But then, as he circled again, he saw a lone figure, lying on a desolate strip of sand. Sam dove down towards it, wondering who it could be.

Sam landed on the sand, several feet from the body, and approached it slowly, his heart pounding. As he reached it, he knelt down.

Hand shaking, he reached out to turn it over. A part of him was in denial, shutting it out—but another part of him, deep down, knew who it was. He sensed her vibration even from here. But he didn't allow himself to believe it could be true.

He turned her over, and everything good that was left within him died.

It was the woman he loved most in the world.

Polly.

Sam grabbed her and pulled her up, holding her, feeling her limp body in his arms. He shook her, trying to revive her. He looked down and saw she had been stabbed in the heart, and that nearly all of her life's force had left her. He felt hot tears pouring down his cheek, as he realized that nothing could possibly save her. There was the slightest flutter in one of her eyes, and he could see that she was still clinging to life.

He hugged her tight, crying over her shoulder, hoping, willing her to come back. Sam couldn't understand how the thing you loved most in the world, at the moment you loved it most, could so suddenly be taken away.

"Sam," he heard her whisper in his ear.

He pulled back and looked at her; it had been so faint, he wondered if she had even spoke.

He put his ear to her mouth.

"I need to tell you something," she whispered again.

Sam felt his heart pounding with remorse, grief, regret. Why hadn't he gotten here sooner? Who could have possibly done this?

But for now, all he wanted was for her to live again. The sight of her like this pained him more than anything he'd ever encountered in his life. He willed for her to come back to him.

"I'm pregnant," Polly whispered into his ear.

Sam's eyes opened wide in shock, as he pulled back and looked at her, wondering if it was true. For the slightest second, a smile crossed her face.

Then, in a flash, it stopped.

Her body went entirely limp, and her eyes opened wide, unblinking.

Sam knew, at that moment, she was dead. He felt it in every pore of his body, as if his own life had just been taken away.

Pregnant. Polly. With his child. Their child.

And now dead.

Both of them.

It was all too much for him to take.

Sam cradled her tight and rocked her, torn apart by anguish, feeling his heart torn to bits.

He leaned back and, fangs extended, roared.

It was a primal roar, one that shook the entire lake, the forest, causing such a vibration that ripples spread across the water and trees shook in their place. It was the sound of a thousand elephants, and it shook the ground itself. As the roar went on and on, it raised the hairs on every beast, on every creature, for a thousand miles.

It was a roar of a creature that had nothing left to live for.

It was a roar of primal fury, of vengeance.

As Sam's eyes watered over, as everything that he loved in the world died within him, a new filter fell over them. It was a filter of violence and bloodlust and revenge. A new spirit, contained deep within him, was now summoned, unleashed. Sam felt it rise up through every pore of his body. It was a spirit of supreme, unstoppable rage. Rage so powerful that it wouldn't discriminate, that it would destroy anything and everything in its path. As Sam snarled, and his eyes turned red, and his fangs lengthened, the muscles in his neck and shoulder bulged, beyond what they'd ever had.

He rose to his feet, holding Polly, and roared again.

It was the roar of an animal that was ready to destroy.

CHAPTER THIRTY ONE

Blake flew with Scarlet in one hand and Ruth in the other, flying as fast as he could to get away from the incoming army. He had been horrified to witness Polly's murder, and shocked to have watched Scarlet taken out that vampire's eye. He had sensed a great disturbance in the area, and had flown there, just to check. He had arrived just at the moment that Polly was stabbed, and when he'd witnessed it, without thinking, he'd dove down and scooped up Scarlet and Ruth. It was too late for Polly, he could see that.

But it was not too late for Scarlet. After all, Scarlet was Caitlin's daughter. And Blake still loved Caitlin. Even if she didn't love him back, he felt there would be no greater way to express his love for her than by rescuing her daughter. Even if it was her daughter with Caleb.

Not that that was his only motivation: Blake would have rescued any helpless child, and in the brief time he had gotten to know her, Blake had fallen in love with Scarlet. She was unusual, advanced beyond her years, and Blake could tell that she would grow into an incredible soul. He knew that saving her would risk his own life, and now, he had an army on his tail. He was vastly outnumbered. He couldn't understand how an entire vampire army could be attacking Skye. There was the ancient vampire law that no coven could attack another by crossing water—unless they were invited. But who would have invited them?

Had Polly? he wondered. After all, she was lying on the beach, dead. But why would she have done such a thing?

Now was not the time to contemplate. Blake put on his fastest speed, and dove for the woods. He knew these woods better than anyone, and as he entered them, he ducked and weaved, twisting and turning, outfoxing the others.

When he was sure he had lost them, he circled back around, and headed back for the castle.

Blake knew he had to get back to the castle, to his own coven, Aiden's men, the King's men, and warn them all. Scarlet and Ruth would be safe inside, and then, between his people and the King's human warriors, they could all fend off the attack. The castle was a ground they could hold, and fortify. He only wished that Caitlin and Caleb were there now, to help them.

Blake burst out of the treeline, and finally the castle came into view. He flew over the footbridge, over the moat, landed in the courtyard before its massive doors, and ran right through them, still holing Scarlet and Ruth. As he was running, a part of him registered that there were no human warriors standing guard outside of it, and that the doors were wide open. He was too flustered to pay it close attention, though; if he hadn't been in such a rush, he would have registered what an ominous sign it was.

Blake screamed out as he ran. "AIDEN!" he shouted. "TAYLOR! TYLER! CAIN! BARBARA!"

He ran room to room, up the stairs, holding Scarlet and Ruth as he took the steps four at a time. He finally made it to the roof.

Several of his coven members were there, gathered together, standing at the parapets and watching the skies with grave concern. He was relieved to see them all here, and also relieved to see Samuel, Caleb's brother, who luckily had been staying here for the wedding. He was also relieved to see dozens of other friendly vampires, those who had come for the wedding and were still here. Blake also counted at least fifty of his own people up there, ready to fight, weapons in hand.

But at the same time, he didn't spot any of McCleod's men, and that concerned him. Blake set Scarlet and Ruth down, and hurried over to the others. He looked everywhere for Aiden, but he was nowhere to be found.

As Blake reached the edge, he looked out at the skies, and saw what the others were all gaping at.

The entire sky was black with an invading vampire army.

Blake was aghast. Even with their dozens of men, there was no way they could possibly defend against all this. This was clearly a well-coordinated, all-out war. Blake was starting to feel unsure even about the safety and security of this castle.

Blake heard a commotion and looked down, and saw with relief that there, below, were hundreds of McCleod's warriors, all with their silver-tip weapons. That was what they needed. Finally, they were coming to help defend the castle.

But Blake's look turned to dismay, as he suddenly realized that these hundreds of warriors were not actually rushing to defend the castle. As McCleod leaned back on his horse and screamed orders at the others, he realized that they all, in full armor, were charging for the castle. As if to attack it.

It was an ambush, Blake realized.

And there was no way out.

CHAPTER THIRTY TWO

Caitlin and Caleb had been flying for hours since they've left Eilean Donan Castle, heading east, across the vast country of Scotland, getting further and further away from the Isle of Skye. Caitlin had not stopped thinking about the moment when they'd opened that chest in Eilean Donan. Inside, sitting there, had been a single, shining, gold key. It was a small key, and seemed to glow with electric energy.

At first, she had wondered if it could be the fourth key. But he had shaken his head, and told her it was different, and she could see that, too. This was one small and gold, whereas the others were large and silver. Caitlin had reached in and picked it up, and examined it in her palm. She'd flipped it over, and spotted a small inscription: "All doors lead to Rosslyn."

Caleb had gasped when he'd heard the phrase.

"Rosslyn," he'd said. "Rosslyn Chapel. Of course. The rumored home to the Holy Grail."

They had not stopped flying since, racing for Rosslyn, the new key sitting in Caitlin's one pocket, and the torn page in her other. Caleb had explained to her along the way that Rosslyn Chapel had been the rumored hiding place of the holy Grail for centuries. Scores of humans and vampires had visited, searching for the Grail. But none had ever been able to find it. It made perfect sense, he said, that her father's clue would lead them there. It was one of the most sacred vampire places in the world.

As they flew now, Caitlin wondered what could be awaiting them. The fourth and final key? Her father himself? The actual Holy Grail? The ancient shield?

And would this be their final stop of the mission?

As they flew, Caitlin couldn't help shaking a persistent feeling of doom. She didn't know why, and she couldn't understand it; but some part of her, deep down, kept telling her that her loved ones were in trouble. Immediately, she thought of Scarlet. Could she be in some kind of danger?

She shook it off. After all, she was also a worried mother now, and it was natural that she would have such anxieties, especially since they were flying in the opposite direction, further and further away from Skye. Caitlin told herself to be strong, not to give in to silly worries. After all, Scarlet was in such good hands, protected by Polly and Sam and Aiden and all the others. What could possibly go wrong?

Besides, they couldn't turn back now, even if they wanted to. There was an urgency to their mission, and the sooner they completed it, the sooner they could be back. And the sooner they found the ancient shield, her father, the more protected Scarlet would be.

After hours of flying, finally, Caitlin sensed the chapel beneath them.

Rosslyn.

Caitlin looked down, and was amazed: this church looked ancient, even for this time, with dozens of narrow, angular spikes rising up along either side of it, lending it an ornate feeling. It was a huge, sprawling structure, built in a dark orange stone, with a sharply sloped, black tiled roof, giving it a look distinct from any other church she had seen. It exuded a certain energy, and Caitlin felt as if she were in the presence of a truly sacred place.

They landed before its entrance, and as they approached it, Caitlin was in awe of everything about this place. It looked like a place of legends. Even its front door was immense, towering over them, with huge, arched doors and a metal knocker. It was embedded in a massive, stone, arched frame, ornately carved. It looked like the entrance to a fairytale.

Caitlin and Caleb exchanged a look, each quietly wondering if they should knock. They reached a silent agreement, and Caitlin stepped forward, grabbed hold of the huge, iron knocker, and slammed it. The sound reverberated throughout the empty courtyard.

No response.

Caitlin slammed it again and again.

They waited, but still no response.

Caitlin had enough of waiting. Finally, she put her shoulder into the door and pushed hard. It was open, but was such a heavy door, she had to push for all she was worth. The door opened slowly, with a creek, and moments later they were inside. Caleb shut the door behind them, and the slam echoed throughout the empty church.

Caitlin was in awe at the sight before her. She had been to some of the greatest churches in the world, and yet this church was different than them all. Built in a reddish stone, it held one of the most ornately designed interiors she had ever seen. Every inch was covered in some shape or design, carved with thousands of symbols, drawings and shapes. Huge, thick columns of stone, the size of tree trunks, filled the nave, rose to the ceiling in arches that curved in every direction, just as thick. This place was clearly built to last. At its far end, the church culminated in an elaborate altar, behind which sat a fifty foot tall, arched stained glass window, showering the room with a soft, muted afternoon light.

With all the signs and symbols carved into the columns and walls and ceiling, Caitlin could not help but wonder what secret messages were hiding here. It was so silent she could hear a pin drop; she sensed she was in the presence of a very sacred place.

"So, you have arrived," came a sudden voice.

Caitlin and Caleb wheeled. Standing there, not ten feet away, was a fellow vampire, dressed in all-white robe, smiling back.

Caitlin wondered how he had managed to get so close so quickly. But, luckily, she did not sense any animosity.

"Rosslyn Chapel," he continued, "burial place for kings and queens for centuries. The site of many a vampire pilgrimage. And the rumored resting place of the Holy Grail."

He stared back at them, smiling.

"But you have not come here to be buried. Or for a pilgrimage. Or to seek the Grail. You are here for something much more special."

He stared, intently studying Caitlin.

"I thought you'd be older," he said with a smile.

Caitlin felt her cheeks reddening; she wasn't sure how to respond. She was caught off guard that he even knew of her at all.

"You have the key?" he asked.

Caitlin slowly nodded back.

Seeming satisfied, he turned and strutted down the long, church aisle.

Caitlin and Caleb exchanged a look, then followed, unsure where he was leading them. As they went, Caitlin felt her heart fluttering, and could feel that they were on the verge of something huge.

Their footsteps echoed as they walked down the empty aisle, reverberating off the ceiling, hundreds of feet high. Caitlin had the odd feeling that there were many eyes on her, although as she looked around the church, surveying the upper balconies, she saw no one.

"People have come to Rosslyn from far and wide, seeking the Grail," the vampire said as he walked, his back still to them. "What they seek, of course, is hidden far beneath us. In the lower crypts. The reason they never find it," he said, stopping before the altar, and facing them, "is because there is no entrance. It was walled off. Centuries ago. And no one knows where to look. Or that it even exists."

He stared intently at Caitlin.

"Your key will reveal it."

He nodded at the altar. Caitlin looked, and saw a tall, golden staff, intricately carved, placed squarely in the altar. At first glance, it looked like an ornate candle holder. But as she looked closely, she could see that it was not. It was an ancient staff, shining in the light, with biblical images carved into it. She could see a tiny hole in it, just big enough to hold a key.

The vampire nodded at her again.

"I hope your key is the right one. We only have one chance at this. If the wrong key is inserted, it will destroy the trail forever. Are you sure it is the right one?"

Caitlin swallowed hard, feeling sweat break out on her forehead. At Eilean Donan, they had only given her one key. She assumed it must be the right one.

Caitlin nodded. She reached up, and slowly inserted the key into the slot. It fit perfectly.

She breathed a sigh of relief.

She gently turned to the right, and as she did, she suddenly heard a rumbling behind her. The staff before her suddenly sank into the ground, lower and lower, and then a wall slid open behind them.

Caitlin was in shock. An ancient passageway had been revealed, clouds of dust coming out of it, leading into the blackness.

The vampire looked at her and smiled. "Well done," he said.

He led the way, taking a torch off the wall, and the three of them walked through the opening and down an ancient, stone stairwell, twisting into the blackness.

They finally reached the lowest levels, and continued down a corridor, barely lit by the torch. Finally, they reached a room.

In it was a single object: a golden stand, on which sat a huge, ancient Bible. The ancient book must have been two feet wide and long, covered in an ornate casing of silver and gold.

The three of them crowded over it. As Caitlin stared, she could feel the scroll heating up in her pocket, and she knew, she just knew, that this was the book from which the page was torn.

Caitlin gently pulled back the heavy pages, surprised at its weight. She turned the pages gingerly, crackling as she went. Each page was thick, and heavy, ancient from years of use, ornately illustrated in all different colors, in drawings all along the edges. The text was in a handwritten scrawl, in ancient Latin. She felt as if she had stepped back into another time.

Caitlin turned and turned, until she reached the middle of the book, and finally, she found it. The torn page. She reached into her pocket, extracted the rolled up scroll, and carefully lined up the other half of the torn page.

It was a perfect match.

They all crowded in closer.

As the pages came together as one, Caitlin could not believe what she saw. Each page showed one half of an ancient shield, sun rays coming off of it, shining. As she lined the pages up together, Caitlin realized it could be none other than a picture of the ancient vampire shield.

All around the picture were Latin words. As the pages lined up, the sentences were now complete. Words, previously torn in half, now fit together, letters matching each other perfectly.

She turned and looked to Caleb. His eyes open wide as he read.

"It's a message," he said, as he scanned the page, reading again and again. "An instruction. It's telling us where to go next. Our final destination. To find the Holy Grail. The final key. And the ancient shield."

He stopped and looked at them both, and Caitlin awaited, breathless, her heart pounding.

"It reads: *the Grail awaits in Dunnottar.*"

CHAPTER THIRTY THREE

Blake could not comprehend the sight unfolding before him. It was one thing to see a vampire army approaching. That was shock enough. But it was quite another to see McCleod's men—the human warriors they had grown to love and to trust—betraying them, attacking them. There was no doubt about it: Blake could see from the scowls on their faces, from the way they were charging, that it was an ambush.

Blake stood on the roof of the castle, with Aiden's men, other vampires he knew and loved—Taylor and Tyler and Caine and Barbara, and scores of others—along with the dozens of other vampires in for the wedding, and knew that there cause was hopeless. They were terribly outnumbered, and the enemy had the advantage of surprise, speed, and superior weaponry. Blake looked around, and wished he saw Polly or Sam somewhere, wished that Caitlin and Caleb were back. But none of them were. They were left on their own, to fend for themselves. The few of them left on the castle rooftop against the thousands of warriors closing in on them by land and by air. Blake was not a pessimist, but he knew a hopeless situation when he saw one.

Still, he prepared to make his stand. He would certainly go down fighting.

But first, he had other priorities. He looked down and saw Scarlet standing there, beside him, and knew that his first order of business was to protect her, to get her out of here. He had to get her far away from the bloodshed that would ensue. Certainly, she would be a casualty otherwise. He also wanted to get her to Caitlin, to have her give her the message that they needed help. That just might save them all. But regardless, more than anything, he owed it to Caitlin to save her only daughter.

Blake jumped into action. He reached down, scooped up Scarlet in one arm and Ruth in the other, and lifted them into the air. He flew away from the oncoming army, over the tops of the human warriors, into the thick mist, then down low into the treetops, where he knew he could lose any pursuers. He flew with all he had, wanting to get Scarlet safely on her way and then get back to help the others.

"Where are you taking me?" Scarlet yelled, struggling, as they flew.

"To safety," Blake yelled back.

"But I don't want to go!" Scarlet argued. "I want to go back to the castle! And help you guys defend it!"

Blake was taken aback by this child's fearlessness. In some ways, she reminded him of Caitlin. But still, he could not give in. Despite her warrior spirit, she would certainly die in any ensuing battle.

Blake soon reached his destination: an ocean beach, on the far eastern side of Skye, down beneath the cliffs. He dove down a cliff he recognized, and aimed right for the rowboat he had stored there, in a cave. He landed right before it, and wasted no time placing Scarlet and Ruth inside the boat.

It was a long, seaworthy, wooden rowboat, with a small sail, and looked like a miniature Viking raiding ship. Blake had used it many times, taking it far out to sea on long voyages. He had liked to sail by himself, late at night, when the ocean was completely empty, letting the waves lap at the boat, and looking up at the moon. He liked to get as far away from others as he could, and let his thoughts wander alone.

Now he could put the boat to good use with Scarlet and Ruth. He could send them off, towards Caitlin.

He leaned over, held Scarlet's shoulders, and looked her in the eye, firmly, mustering all the intensity he could to try to convince this strong-willed girl.

"You are a brave little girl," Blake said. "You are fearless. I know that. And there's no other little girl in the world that I would ask to do this. But I know you're special. I know that you can handle it. Am I right?"

Blake had sensed her pride, her fearlessness, and he wanted to appeal to it.

He was happy to see it work. She lifted her head up tall, proudly, and nodded her head solemnly.

"Good," he said. "I'm sending you on a voyage, to your mother and father. You have a special power, a special bond with them. The sea will take you right to them. If you focus. Use your power. Close your eyes as you sail, and let the universe guide you to exactly where you need to go. You are a powerful child. You can make it happen. Can you do that for me?"

Scarlet nodded back, but seemed unsure.

"But what if it takes me to the wrong place?" she asked. "What if I don't end up near my Mommy?"

"You will. You could end up in no other place. The vampire connection is too strong. Only focus on her. And don't let go."

Blake was about to turn and, when suddenly, he remembered something. He reached into his pocket and extracted something he'd been meaning to give to Caitlin for centuries. He took Scarlet's little hand, opened it, and placed it in her palm.

Scarlet looked down, eyes open in wonder.

It was a small piece of sea glass. A piece of the sea glass he had given her centuries ago, in Pollepel.

"Please give it to her," he said "and tell her I will always love her."

And with that, Blake suddenly leaned down, grabbed the hull and give it a huge heave into the ocean. Within moments, the small sail caught, and the current took the boat out, already far from shore.

Blake saw Scarlet stand in the boat and look back at him, fear momentarily crossing her eyes.

Blake raised a fist into the air, holding it up high over his head. It was a gesture of confidence, to tell her that she could make it.

After a moment's hesitation, Scarlet raised her fist in the air, and returned the gesture.

Blake turned, took three strides, and leapt into the air.

Now he had a war to wage.

CHAPTER THIRTY FOUR

Blake raced back to the castle, flying faster than he ever had, eager to get back and help his people. Now that Scarlet was safe, Blake turned all his attention towards helping the others.

As he reached the castle, he looked down and saw complete mayhem: it was an all-out war, as hundreds of vampires battled each other below. His people were terribly outnumbered, attacked from all sides, and Blake was crestfallen to see that, with the battle barely begun, several of his people were already dead, their bodies thrown over the edge of the castle.

Simultaneously, Blake could see there was another battle going on below, on the castle grounds, before the entrance. This battlefront was being led by Kyle and by McCleod. Together, they were relentlessly killing all those who tried to flee. It was an ambush, and there was nowhere to go.

It was all happening so fast, at vampire speed, in the blink of an eye. As Blake flew for just a few seconds, debating where best to land, he already saw so many things happening at once: on the rooftop, he flinched as he saw Rynd step up and murder Taylor, stabbing her in the back, and through the heart, as she faced off with other vampires. He heard her scream, and watched her life force depart from her.

At the same time, down below, Kyle stepped up and surprised her twin brother, Tyler, putting his sword through his heart, and killing him on the spot. Blake was breathless. The two twins, who he had known and loved for centuries, now dead in a matter of moments, killed at the hands of Rynd and Kyle.

In the same instant, McCleod charged on his horse, up behind Barbara, swung his axe, and chopped off her head in a single blow. Aiden's men were being wiped out faster than Blake could even take in.

There were a few signs of hope. One of them was Samuel, Caleb's brother. Blake watched in admiration as Samuel fearlessly fought off hordes of Kyle's men, down below. He seemed to be as good a fighter as his brother, and few vampires were able to get close to him.

As Blake watched, Samuel faced off with McCleod. They each drew long swords, and a crowd gathered around to watch. Their swords clanged, left and right, as they faced off, swung and parried. Neither gave an inch, both seasoned veterans, and for a moment, it seemed as if it might end in a stalemate.

But then, suddenly, Samuel spun around, holding out his sword, and in an unexpected move, he surprised the King, and in one quick motion, he chopped off his head with his silver sword.

For a moment, the body remained in place; then, it slumped and collapsed to the ground, and his head went rolling. The crowd of McCleod's men let out a horrified gasp, too surprised to react.

As Blake watched, he saw Sera suddenly appear, out of the shadows, waiting for her moment. She stepped up behind Samuel with a silver dagger, and raised it high. Blake could see that she was about to plunge it into his neck.

Blake sprang into action. He dove down, aiming right for the dagger, using every ounce of his will to get there as fast as he could. He sped through the air, hand out, and reached it at the very last second. As the tip of the knife was a millimeter from Samuel's neck, Blake managed to grab Sera's wrist, and tackle her to the ground.

On the ground, wrestling with Sera, in the thick of all the fighting, Blake felt himself get kneed hard in the solo plexus. Sera had managed to lift her knee, and knock the wind out of him.

Blake rolled on his side, and before he could catch his breath, he found himself kicked in the face by several other vampires, falling on him like ants.

But Blake also noticed that Sera had dropped her dagger, and in one motion, he managed to roll over, snatch it, roll one more time, and then take a knee and throw it, hoping his aim was perfect.

It was. Sera had not expected it, and the dagger lodged perfectly in her throat. Seconds later, she collapsed, eyes wide open in shock. Blake watched her fall, finally, dead.

But Sera and McCleod were but minor victories. Blake was still terribly outnumbered, as was Samuel, and with every passing second, dozens more vampires pounced on them. Blake found himself getting kicked and punched left and right.

As he stumbled back, trying to fight off ten men at once, trying to catch his breath, the other vampires suddenly parted ways for Rynd, who now faced off with him. Blake squared off, while at the same time, he noticed that Samuel, several feet away, was squaring off with Kyle.

Blake went blow for blow with Rynd, using long swords and shields; but he was no match, he knew, for Rynd's evil power. Rynd was too well-rested, too fast, too strong, too treacherous. And Blake could see, out of the corner of his eye, that Samuel was not doing much better. Kyle had him, too, on the ropes.

Blake felt himself losing with each passing blow, and knew that it would only be a matter of minutes until he, and Samuel, were both dead. He only prayed that his final moments could be his most valiant ones on earth.

Suddenly, Blake sensed a disturbance in the crowd. There was a murmur, then agitation, and then he noticed scores of the enemy start to run, to scurry away.

Blake could not understand what was happening. Until finally, he saw what it was.

Approaching the battlefield was Caitlin's brother. Sam. Blake could not believe it. He had never seen anyone look so embittered, so vicious. He didn't even recognize him. Sam looked like a man possessed, like he had been to the depths of hell and back. He fought with a power and courage and ferocity that Blake had never before witnessed. He sliced through vampire after vampires as if slicing through butter, leaving a trail of dead bodies in his wake. He was cutting his way through the crowd, and heading right for Rynd. And he had a deadly vengeance in his eyes.

Not a moment too soon for Blake. Rynd brought down a vicious blow, right for Blake's head, and Blake held up his own sword with two hands, blocking it. He held the sword at bay, just inches from his face. But Rynd's sword was inching lower, and Blake knew that he had but seconds left to live.

But that was all he needed. Sam cut his way through the crowd and reached Rynd just in time, kicking him so hard that Rynd went flying like a ragdoll across the field.

Blake, grateful, wanted to thank Sam. But he saw that he couldn't: Sam's face was like that of a wild animal, not even recognizable, and Blake felt scared just looking at it. In fact, Blake wanted to run, and knew he should get out of Sam's path. But he was frozen in fear, and he had to see what happened next.

Blake looked over and saw that Rynd, upon looking up at Sam, was terrified, too. He never thought he would see a creature like Rynd be scared of anything—but the look on Sam's face had done it to him. Blake wondered what could have happened to Sam to make him like this.

And then he remembered: Polly. Sam was on a path of vengeance.

Sam took three huge steps, and raised his sword high, right for Rynd.

Rynd held up his own sword to block it, but Sam brought down his sword with such power that it cut Rynd's sword clean in half.

Rynd, shocked, looked up at his own sword in wonder.

Sam then leaned back and kicked Rynd's wrist, sending the hilt of his sword flying, and in the same motion, kicked Rynd hard in the chest, sending him flying back and crashing into the stone wall of the castle.

Without missing a beat, Sam stepped up, grabbed Rynd by the hair, and smashed his head into the stone wall repeatedly, again and again and again. Rynd was helpless in Sam's grip.

In moments, Rynd was near dead. But Sam was not finished. He hoisted Rynd up high over his shoulders, and then in two leaps, he jumped to the top of the castle parapets. Blake was shocked. It must have been at least a hundred feet, yet Sam did it effortlessly. Then Sam jumped, holding Rynd, off the roof, and aimed right for the huge lance implanted at the entranceway. He impaled Rynd's body through it, right through his heart. Rynd's body slid all the way through the lance, down to the base, killing him instantly.

Rynd's body sat there, impaled on the lance for all eyes to see, as Sam stood over him.

But Sam wasn't done yet. Whatever rage was driving him hadn't been satisfied. Sam looked left and right, snarling, like a wild animal ready to kill anything in its path.

Seeing the look on Sam's face, Blake finally summoned the courage to flee, and he saw that Samuel did, too. All of Rynd's men were fleeing, too, as were all of McCleod's men. Apparently, with their leaders dead and a monster on the prowl, none of them wanted to linger any longer. They fled into the sky, over the lake, back from where they'd come, and they could not move fast enough.

Within moments, the entire battlefield had cleared out.

Except, that is, for Sam.

And one other: Kyle.

CHAPTER THIRTY FIVE

Kyle had been having a field day. He hadn't had this much fun in centuries, slaughtering Aiden's men left and right. It had been a route.

It had been especially fun stabbing Taylor through the heart, watching her die slowly at his feet. These silvertip weapons were the strongest and most effective he had ever wielded, and after killing Taylor, he had killed a dozen more vampires in just a few minutes. He was covered in their blood, and he smiled widely, beginning to feel himself again.

Their plan had worked perfectly, and Kyle knew that in no time, they would wipe out every last one of them. They had them surrounded, outnumbered, and it had been a slaughter fest. Rynd's shapeshifting trick had worked, as Kyle knew it would, and that girl Polly had been stupid enough to fall for the bait. Now, there was nothing left to stand in his way. With all of these vampires dead, it would only be a matter of time until they cornered and slaughtered Caitlin and Caleb.

Kyle's latest victim, in his sights, would be Samuel, Caleb's brother. Samuel was strong, but he was too outnumbered, and beaten down, and Kyle had him on the defense. The more they fought, the more confident Kyle became, and Kyle knew that in just moments, Samuel would be finished.

That was when the disruption began. Kyle didn't understand what was going on, but suddenly, all of their men had begun fleeing, running for their lives, as if scared of an incoming attack. And just as Kyle had been about to plunge his sword into Samuel's chest, that was when he stopped and saw it.

Kyle turned and was amazed to see Sam, Caitlin's brother, approaching the battlefield like a madman. He had never seen anything like it, anyone fighting so quickly, so powerfully. It was like a whirlwind. Kyle had seen rage throughout the centuries, but he had never seen rage like this. This was the rage of a creature that had nothing left to lose. That wanted to die.

Sam was a one-man disruptive force. He was slaughtering Rynd's men as if they were dolls, and as Kyle watched in horror, Sam squared off with Rynd, and within moments, killed him, impaling him on that lance.

That was when everyone else on the battlefield fled. Everyone. Even Aiden's men. Sam was clearly not distinguishing between good and bad. He was simply killing anything and everything in his path.

For a moment, Kyle thought about fleeing himself.

But then he decided otherwise. Kyle had enough of running. Now, he figured, was time to stop and fight. To make a final stand. If Kyle was going to die, this was the time and place he wanted to go out. After all, he had vowed to make this time and place his last, had vowed that if he couldn't kill Caitlin and her people now, then he would die trying. There would be no more chasing, no more going back in time for him.

And now it was time to die trying.

*

Sam approached the battlefield in a rage so white-hot, he could barely see, barely distinguish what he was doing. Sam had never experienced anything like it before: his rage was so consuming, so overwhelming, he felt it lifting him into its grip, taking him over as a force of its own. He couldn't control it if he tried.

Instead, he let it consume him. It moved his arms and legs, dictated who and how he should fight. Since Polly's death, Sam had nothing left to live for. All he had left in him was to destroy. To avenge. And anyone and everything in his path would pay the price for being alive on this planet while Polly was not.

Sam had enjoyed killing Rynd. As he jumped off the roof with him, and impaled him through that lance, he had felt a shiver of electricity run through his body, felt Polly watching him from above, appreciating the vengeance he got for her. He was beginning to feel satisfied.

But he was nowhere near done. He looked for someone or something else to fight, and he was dismayed to see everyone fleeing from him, as if he were some sort of monster. But there was one creature that stood still and faced him, Sam was delighted to see.

And he was even happier to see who was: Kyle. The disgusting, disfigured, mutated Kyle. The arch enemy of his sister, the being who had so tortured and pursued them throughout the centuries. The very creature who had captured Sam himself, back in New York City, and who was responsible for Samantha turning him in the first place. The man who had tricked him into using shapeshifting against his own sister.

Sam smiled with delicious delight. He squared off with Kyle, and tossed his heavy longsword from hand-to-hand as if it weighed nothing. This was a battle he relished.

Sam wasted no time. A split second later, he brought his sword down with two hands right for Kyle's head, with enough force to slice him in two, several times over. To Sam's surprise, Kyle managed to raise his own sword and to block the blow just in time. Kyle was quicker than Sam thought.

But he was still no match for Sam. The power of Sam's strike cut Kyle's sword clean in half. Kyle looked down at his sword, clearly shocked that anything had enough force to do that.

Sam didn't hesitate. He reached up and kicked Kyle's shield square on, smashing it into Kyle's face, and sending Kyle flying back through the air, thirty feet, and landing on the dirt.

In a flash, Sam was already on top of him, grabbing him, spinning him, and tossing him like a ragdoll through the open-air, smashing him hard into the stone wall of the castle.

Kyle, dazed and confused, outmatched, looked up at Sam through bleary eyes, as if wondering how anyone could move that fast, have that much power. Kyle slowly rose to his feet, but Sam was already there again, and kicked him with such force that it sent him back another thirty feet, and smashing right through the castle wall.

Before Kyle could even think to sit up again, Sam was already on top of him, with a knee on his chest, pinning him to the ground. Sam looked down at this pathetic creature in disgust.

He reached back and extracted the dagger that was used to kill Polly, the one he had found near her body.

"Any final words before I send you to hell?" Sam snarled, through gritted teeth

Kyle snarled back up, blood oozing from his mouth, gasping for air, and locked eyes on Sam's.

"I only wish that I was the one who had killed Polly," Kyle spat, with a bloody grin. "I heard she died slowly and painfully."

Sam snarled, raised the dagger high, and brought it down right into Kyle's heart.

As he did, Sam felt a tremendous rumbling in the universe, felt the ground beneath him shake. He watched as shadows of dozens of small black demons appeared, hovered over Kyle's lifeless body. He watched as they grappled with the black spirit leaving Kyle's body, as they carted it off down below, beneath the ground, towards the depths of hell. This was followed by a huge flash of purple light, and suddenly, Kyle's body disintegrated before Sam's eyes, first rocketing up to the clouds, then turning down and shooting beneath the earth.

It was an epic death, and it was clear to Sam that a huge force had just been extinguished in the universe.

At the same moment, as Sam watched, a part of the black spirit that had left Kyle's body at death, suddenly rose up, and descended over him. Sam felt it covering him, creep into his bones and settle there. Sam vaguely remembered once being told that, when one kills someone of such evil, there was a danger of taking on his spirit. Of becoming as evil as him.

Despite his best efforts, Sam felt himself transforming, becoming something that he wasn't. Veins bulging from his neck, Sam felt that he was, inevitably, inextricably, being infused with a new, evil spirit. He felt that he was turning to the dark side. And as he leaned back and roared, he knew, he just knew, that there was no way he could ever turn back again.

CHAPTER THIRTY SIX

Caitlin and Caleb flew through the late afternoon sky, heading north up the coast of Scotland, heading to Dunnottar Castle. Caitlin's heart was pounding as they went. Here they were, just moments away from their final destination, from finding the fourth and final key, from finding the Holy Grail itself. She felt closer than she ever had to her father, felt as if he were just a stone's throw away. She could, finally, feel her journey, her mission, coming to a close. She felt excited and relieved and nervous at the same time. Would he be there, waiting to greet her? Would he have the vampire shield waiting?

As Caitlin flew, holding Caleb's hand, she reflected on their whirlwind journey through Scotland. Dunvegan Castle, Skye, Eilean Donan, Rosslyn Chapel…She kept seeing in her mind's eye that huge, ancient Bible in the crypts of Rosslyn, kept seeing the image of the shield as the two pages became one. The clue had been so well guarded and protected, each place offering just the smallest hint of where to go.

But now it was all finally coming together, and Caitlin felt for certain that this was the final stop.

After hours of flying, the landscape finally changed, as they flew along the edge of the Scottish coast. And as they rounded a bend, a castle came into view, one that Caitlin knew could only be Dunnottar.

The site took Caitlin's breath away. She had never seen anything like it: it was the most remote and picturesque castle she had ever seen. Built on the very edge of a cliff which dropped hundreds of feet straight down to the ocean, the castle sat proudly at the edge of a small, green island, soaring high up in the air, partially in the clouds, as if reaching for heaven itself. The small island, just big enough to hold the castle, was connected to the mainland only by a narrow strip of land. It was the most well defended site Caitlin had ever seen. Surrounded by steep cliffs and water on all sides, no one could dare approach it. The only other way in or out was a narrow strip of land connecting it to the mainland, a bottleneck, easily defendable, with sharp cliffs dropping off on either side.

Dunnottar castle itself was a beautiful, sprawling piece of architecture, with round parapets and a large, quadrangular inner courtyard. Partially hidden in mist, it looked like something out of one of Caitlin's dreams. It was a mystical, magical place, and if there was anything powerful left to be found, clearly this was the place to find it.

Caitlin looked at Caleb, and could see he was equally impressed by the sight. They circled again and again, taking it all in from above, getting a bird's eye view. No matter how many times she circled it, Caitlin was awestruck, from every angle.

As they tried flying closer, Caitlin felt an invisible shield keeping them at bay. Clearly, vampires could not fly directly into the castle, or even onto the island itself; they would have to land on the mainland, and walk across the narrow strip of land. This must be, Caitlin realized, a very well-defended vampire fortress. She only hoped that the vampires here were friendly.

Caitlin and Caleb landed at the base of the long strip of land leading to the island. Covered in slippery moss, freshly wet from the spray of ocean waves, and with steep cliffs falling off on either side, they held each other's hands as they walked, careful not to slip. The sound of the ocean waves crashing far below was overpowering, and Caitlin could feel the spray in the wind.

As they approached, on foot, the castle looked even more imposing. Caitlin couldn't spot anyone. This place seemed to be completely, eerily, deserted.

But she knew they were in the right place. She felt it. There was no other place they could possibly be. She could feel the three other keys throbbing in her pocket, and she knew they were guiding her, telling her that she was about to have the fourth.

Caitlin and Caleb crossed the land just as the sun was beginning to set, covering the sky in pink and red. It was a staggeringly beautiful site, and Caitlin felt as if she were on top of the world. She was on guard the entire time she crossed, ready for an ambush. Luckily, none came.

They finished crossing, and stood on the small island, before the castle. Together, they approached the imposing, ancient stone wall, walking right up to the massive wooden door. The door must have stood fifty feet high, dwarfing them. Caitlin looked up at the huge metal knocker, then looked to Caleb.

He nodded back.

"If they are for us, they will answer," Caleb said. "If not, they will know we're here anyway."

Caitlin agreed silently, and was about to reach up and grab the ring.

But at just that moment, something caught her eye, something in the distance. At first, she thought she was imagining it. But then, she turned her head and looked more carefully.

There, down in the distance, hundreds of feet below, bobbing in the water, was something. Caitlin felt sure of it.

She turned and walked to the edge of the cliff, looking down, shielding her eyes from the glare. Caleb came up beside her, slipping his arm around her waist.

"What is it?" he asked.

At first, Caitlin sensed more than saw something, but finally, something came into view. There, in the distance, bobbing in the ocean waves. A small boat. Like a rowboat, with a small sail.

Caitlin's heart stopped. Every pore in her body told her who was in that boat.

Scarlet.

Without hesitating, Caitlin jumped and dove straight down off the cliff, hoping her wings would take. She plummeted to earth at a thousand miles an hour, and, at the last second, her wings finally took, and she soared in a clean arc, gliding right out to sea, Caleb right behind her.

Without pausing, Caitlin swooped down, picked up Scarlet, held her in her arms, and continued to fly. Right behind her, Caleb scooped up Ruth.

Caitlin hugged Scarlet tightly, and she hugged her back; as she did, Caitlin could feel her shaking over her shoulder. The child was definitely shaken up, and Caitlin had absolutely no idea what she was doing out there, alone, in the middle of the ocean. Why was she in the boat, by herself, the middle of the sea? And heading towards her? How was it possible? Especially after Polly and Sam had vowed that they would watch over her?

Suddenly, Caitlin was overcome with dread, as she realized there was no possible way they would have left her alone, have set her out to sea, unless something terrible had happened to them. But what?

They flew up the cliff, landing back where they had started, right before the entrance to the castle. Caitlin set Scarlet down, as Caleb set Ruth down, and Caitlin brushed the hair out of Scarlet's eyes, trying to calm her as she cried.

Caitlin knelt down, leaned in and kissed her on her forehead.

"Shhh," Caitlin whispered, stroking her hair. "It's all right. Everything is all right now. Tell Mommy what happened."

"He put me in a boat," Scarlet began, crying, "with Ruth. I wanted to stay and fight. But he said I had to go. Then he pushed the boat into the ocean. He said it would take me to you."

"Who?" Caitlin asked, confused.

But Scarlet began crying again, and only held out her little fist, as if to hand her something. Caitlin reached out, and Scarlet dropped a small piece of sea glass into her hand.

Caleb was at first puzzled—and then she realized. There was only one person in the world who would have given her this glass.

"He told me to tell you that he loves you," Scarlet added.

Caitlin felt as if a knife had plunged into her heart. Blake. He had saved Scarlet. He had put her in the boat, sent her off. She felt more indebted to him than she ever had.

But saved Scarlet from what? That was the question.

"From an army," came the voice, answering her silent question.

Caitlin stood and spun, as did Caleb, and was shocked to see, standing a few feet away, Aiden. He stood there, his back against the open sky, wearing his white robe, holding his staff, and staring at her with grave concern. As always, he had appeared at the most uncanny moment.

"What army?" Caitlin asked, feeling terribly guilty already that she had left, that she hadn't been there to help protect Scarlet, Polly, her brother and whoever else.

"It was Kyle's work. And Rynd's. And Sera's. They sabotaged and surprised our people. There was little they could do."

Caitlin felt the wind knocked out of her, her feeling of dread confirmed. She felt more grateful than ever that Scarlet had made it out alive. But she wondered who else might not have been so lucky.

"Was anyone…hurt?" Caitlin asked, already knowing it was a stupid question.

Aiden nodded gravely. Caitlin braced herself for his response.

"Many of our finest are dead. Taylor. Tyler. Cain. Barbara. And, I'm sorry to say, Polly."

Caitlin felt herself week in the knees, sinking into the earth. Polly. Her best friend. Practically, her sister. One of few people she had come to care for most in the world. Her future sister in law. Dead.

Polly.

All while she, Caitlin, was away. Caitlin couldn't possibly feel worse.

Then she remembered the others. Blake. And Sam.

"And what of the others?" Caitlin was afraid to know. "My brother?"

Aiden paused, a long, serious pause, and that silence terrified her more than any news. She already knew that, whatever it was, it wasn't good.

"I'm afraid we have lost him," Aiden finally said. "Not to death. But to the dark side."

Caitlin was bewildered.

"Our men are not the only ones who have died on this day. Kyle, too, is dead. So is Rynd. And Sera. But there was a high price to pay for this. Sam has crossed to the dark side in rage and vengeance. It is a path from which he can never return. He is lost to us. The brother you once knew is no more."

Caitlin felt herself sinking, spiraling down, her whole world becoming black. She felt as if she were about to collapse. She didn't know if any worse news could come on this day. She suddenly had the desire to fly off into the horizon, to go back to Skye, to do whatever she could.

Aiden read her mind, and shook his head.

"There's nothing you can do. It is too late. You see, this was all destined. Pre-ordained. Your purpose is to finish the mission. We all count on you."

"But there is no one left," Caitlin said, weakly.

"You're wrong. Many are left. And when you find the shield, it just might be our only hope to bring the others back."

Caitlin hesitated, unsure if she could go on anymore.

Aiden stepped forward and stared at her intently, looking deep into her eyes.

"You vowed," he said. "You vowed that no matter what, you would go on. I told you it would not be easy. I told you something would be taken away from you. But you made a promise. And now it is time for you to fulfill your promise."

Aiden took two steps forward, reached up on the iron knocker, and slammed it twice. Then he stood to the side, as the sound echoed throughout the empty courtyard.

Finally, the ancient door slowly opened.

Standing there, staring back, were a dozen vampires, all old men, with long white beards, and all dressed in white. They nodded at Aiden, who nodded back. Then they parted ways, and gestured for Caitlin and Caleb to follow.

It took all of Caitlin's will to force herself to take the first step.

*

As they all walked into the castle, following the vampires, Caitlin knew that they were in the right place. She could feel her father so close, as if he were just beyond the next door.

They followed silently down an ancient stone corridor, twisting and turning, single file. They came to a large doorway, and the door opened, revealing a large, interior courtyard.

Caitlin took in her surroundings in awe: the soft grass of the inner courtyard was lit up in the sunset, and a beautiful rose light descended over the ancient stone walls. Even more startling, in the courtyard were hundreds of vampires, all along its walls, dressed in all white, standing at attention, waiting silently.

Caitlin felt a hundred eyes on her as they walked to the center of the large, triangular courtyard.

They approached three vampires who stood apart from the others, in the center, staring at them. The one in the middle held a small, golden chest. The vampires on either side of him each held a golden goblet, filled, Caitlin could see, with a white liquid.

She looked everywhere for a sign of her father. She wondered if any of these men could be him. But she didn't see him. Caitlin stopped right before the center vampire, and as they waited, she could hear a pin drop. The only sound was the whipping of the wind in this remote place, whistling over the grass, over the ancient walls.

"Caitlin of the Pollepel Coven," pronounced the vampire in the middle, staring down at her. "You have done well. We are proud of you. And so is your father."

"Is he here?" Caitlin asked.

Slowly, the man shook his head.

"Your father lives in another time and place," he answered. "Before you can see him, you first need all four keys. We are the guardians of the fourth and final key. The key that you will need to see him, and to save us all."

The man lifted up the golden box and held it before Caitlin.

"Your key," he said.

Caitlin looked at him, and noticed that he was looking to the base of her throat.

She reached up, and felt the small antique cross around her neck. She marveled at how many times she had taken this with her, how many places, at how many keys it had unlocked. She held it out one last time, hoping it would fit, and inserted it into the small, golden chest.

To her surprise, the key fit. The chest opened with a soft click.

Sitting there, inside the red velvet, was a large, silver key. It was identical to the other three keys in her pocket.

She could hardly believe it. The fourth and final key.

She reached in and slowly extracted it, feeling it in her palm.

"One final time," the man said. "You will be sent back one final time. And in the next time and place, you will use your four keys. And you will meet your father."

The man nodded, and the other two vampires stepped forward, each holding out a goblet. Caitlin looked at the white liquid.

"The Holy Grail?" Caitlin asked, nervous.

The vampire shook his head.

"Your father holds the Holy Grail. He and no one else."

Caitlin reached up and held the goblet, and looked over and saw Caleb did the same. They exchanged a look, and at the same time, they lifted the liquid to their lips.

The hundreds of vampires crowded in close, all around them, forming a small, tight circle, all holding hands. They began to chant, at first a soft noise, then their words rose, soon becoming louder than the waves.

"We hereby lay thee down to rest, Caitlin, Caleb, and Scarlet, to resurrect another day, in God's ultimate grace."

Caitlin reached out and took Caleb's had in one hand, and Scarlet's in the other. She thought of all the darkness and destruction that had overcome all those close to her—Sam, Polly, Blake, and all the others—and she struggled to push away her overwhelming sadness. As she tried to put it out of her mind, her world became lighter from the liquid, and soon, she felt herself growing so light. She knew that in moments, when she opened her eyes, she would be in another time and place. The final time and place.

She only hoped that her father would be there, waiting.

COMING SOON...

Book #8 in the Vampire Journals

Please visit Morgan's site, where you can join the mailing list, hear the latest news, see additional images, and find links to stay in touch with Morgan on Facebook, Twitter, Goodreads and elsewhere:

www.morganricebooks.com

Also by Morgan Rice

turned
(book #1 in the Vampire Journals)

loved
(Book #2 in the Vampire Journals)

betrayed
(Book #3 in the Vampire Journals)

destined
(Book #4 in the Vampire Journals)

desired
(Book #5 in the Vampire Journals)

betrothed
(Book #6 in the Vampire Journals)